The Nanny's Secret

An absolutely addictive psychological thriller with a jaw-dropping twist

SL Harker

Copyright © 2023 by SL Harker

All rights reserved.

No part of this book may be reproduced in any form or by any electronic or mechanical means, including information storage and retrieval systems, without written permission from the author, except for the use of brief quotations in a book review.

Chapter 1

Afternoon sunlight travels across the face of the young woman sitting at the breakfast bar. My nanny candidate, Holly Goodwin, is a smiley twenty-something with her hands clasped tightly together. She squints slightly against the bright light. The flash of yellow brings out the amber hues of her light-brown hair worn impeccably straight to her shoulders.

She sits primly. Her smile is small and knowing.

Wearing a simple navy hair band and pearl stud earrings, she reminds me of uptight soccer moms who bring extra orange slices to the games. Holly straightens her shoulders, her eyes sparkling with enthusiasm.

"Oh, I don't mind a fussy baby," she says. Her voice is soft and honey sweet. "My last family hired me after they had trouble with their newborn. I stayed with them for two years in the end. It's always hard to leave, but they'd only planned to hire me for six months. Mrs. Watson still sends me updates, along with little Sawyer's crayon drawings."

I lean in, giving her a quick, professional smile. I don't want to seem too keen, even though on the inside I'm silently thanking the universe for bringing her to us. With help, I can return to my floral shop. I can get out of the house that has been stifling me. God knows I'm going stir-crazy here. "Holly, I think it's safe to say that you are smart, qualified, and have great references. I love my shop, and I'm excited about returning, but it's bittersweet, you know? I want to put my family in the care of someone I can trust."

"That's completely understandable," she says. She bites her lip slightly as though in anticipation.

"I'm certain that person is you." I smile.

Holly's pale-blue eyes grow wider and wider. Her cheeks flush slightly. She shifts to the edge of her seat. "Really?"

Before I can answer, the door leading to the garage bursts open. Jace, my twelve-year-old son, files in first, his baseball cleats clomping across the tiles. Two sand-colored patches rest on the knees of his baseball uniform.

"Jace, shoes, honey." I point to them, standing.

Holly stands, too, a confident smile stretching her lips. She folds her hands together, waiting for an introduction.

"Sorry, Mom." Jace rolls his eyes and uses the toe of one cleat to shove off the other shoe.

Behind him, my husband, Rick, steps into the house, our six-month-old baby planted on his right hip. He's as handsome as always, and seeing him with little Lissa makes my stomach tingle.

His eyes find mine first then Holly's. He immediately puts out a free hand. "Rick Miller."

The Nanny's Secret

"Hi, I'm Holly. Holly Goodwin." Her eyes briefly meet my husband's gaze before flicking down to her sensible shoes.

"Am I too late?" Rick asks, his eyes panning between us, his brows knitting together. "Sorry, practice went on longer than normal." He glances at Jace, who stomps over to the fridge.

"It wasn't my fault. I'm not the coach," Jace says.

I give Holly an apologetic smile. "Sorry. This is what having a preteen is like."

Jace sulks behind the refrigerator door.

"That's okay. What team are you on?" she asks, raising her voice so Jace can hear her.

He slowly closes the fridge door and stares at her, a little dumbfounded.

"Um... the Knights." He slides a hand behind his head and rubs his fingers across the nape of his neck.

"That's cool. I love baseball. The Yankees are my favorite team."

A twitch of a smile creases at the edge of Jace's lips. "No way."

"You like them?" Holly keeps her focus on him.

"They're my favorite too."

"Yeah?" Holly's voice perks up. "Maybe we can talk sports some time. What position do you play?"

"Shortstop."

"Just like Jeter did." Holly flashes Jace a vibrant smile, showing off a row of perfect white teeth.

Jace grins, twisting the cap off his water bottle. "Yeah. Um. That's cool."

"Be careful what you wish for. Jace will talk your ear off about baseball," Rick says with a chuckle.

A swell of happiness gathers in my abdomen. This is going to work, I realize. Holly is perfect for us. She fits right in. And all my problems, all those dark thoughts on the edges of my mind, will be eased. Finally.

Rick kisses me on the cheek and gently passes me baby Lissa. I bounce her a couple times, pressing my face into her neck to relish the lingering lavender scent of her bath soap.

I squeeze her tiny, dimpled hand. "This is Holly. Do you want her to be your new nanny?"

Rick's eyebrows rise. "That fast, huh?"

"I don't think we need to interview anyone else." I crane my head toward Jace. "What do you think?"

He shifts his weight and stares at the floor. "Sounds good to me."

"Thank you so much, Mrs. Miller. You won't regret it, I promise," Holly says. There's a note of relief in her voice. It gives me pause. I wonder how desperate she is for a job. Something about that makes my skin prickle with discomfort at the thought.

I ignore my worries and bat a hand, dismissing her formalities. "Please. Call me Audrey. We'll be family in no time. Especially if you'll be living here."

"Rick is good for me," my husband says, always quick to roll with the punches. "Audrey is fantastic at reading people. So you're going to fit right in here."

I slip my free arm around Rick's waist. The fact that he trusts my instincts makes me so happy.

The Nanny's Secret

But it also makes me feel guilty.

Before my thoughts turn cloudy, Lissa squeals and claps her chubby hands together, as if to give her stamp of approval too.

"I think she likes you already," Rick says.

"May I hold her?" Holly asks.

"Of course." Gently, I hand Lissa over to Holly, watching as Holly easily rests her against her hip.

"Better get used to it. She loves cuddles," Rick says with a chuckle.

"Well, who doesn't?" Holly coos, bouncing Lissa.

I glance between Rick and Holly. For a fleeting second, I wonder whether I'm making a mistake to hire a nanny who is so well put together and—dare I even say it?—pretty, but I trust Rick. And I should give Holly the benefit of the doubt. She's perfectly pleasant and sweet. If she can get Jace engaged in conversation, that's a win in my book, and she's clearly great with babies.

Still, this is a live-in nanny position, and I've heard my fair share of horror stories about how the nanny steals the husband. Rick isn't like that. He's never cheated on me before with someone younger or prettier. Why would he start now?

A sour, sickly sensation prickles at my insides. No, Rick would never cheat on me. But trust has been broken between us before. I push the thought away and force myself to smile.

I hold out my hand to our new nanny. "Holly, if you want the job, it's yours."

Chapter 2

"You really have a knack for floral décor, Mrs. Miller." Holly halts in the foyer, where I have a bouquet of fresh stargazer lilies arranged with purple tulips. I've chosen a simple clear glass vase to put them in, and the vase is perched on a table against the wall. "And it smells divine."

It's the next day, and Holly has returned to our quiet residential street, bags in tow, ready to move into our home.

"Please, it's Audrey. Mrs. Miller makes me feel too"—I trail off, my fingers fluttering to my collarbone—"old or something." I look at this girl, who is almost twenty years younger than me, and try to imagine who I was at her age. Lost, most probably. A nightmare for my parents as I drifted away from the idea of college. Working part-time as a waitress who downed shots with the busboys after a long shift.

Luckily, I met Rick not long after and put all that behind me. I'd wanted to be a better woman for him. He wasn't just handsome. He was solid. A stand-up, loyal guy from a good family. I'd needed to step up, and I did. I stepped so far up that it made me fall harder when I messed up.

Holly's eyes crinkle at the corners. Her smile is genuine when she says, "Don't be silly. You look fantastic. Not old at all."

I study her for a moment—her fresh, youthful features, the natural rosiness of her cheeks, the gloss of her brown hair. I'm trying not to compare myself to her, but it's almost instinctual. My hair needs a refresh. The gray roots are poking through my blond highlights. The skin under my eyes is turning papery and no longer takes well to concealer. But without the makeup, my dark circles frame my brown eyes. Of course I compare myself to her. She's in her prime. I'm past mine. But I refuse to allow jealousy to creep into my thoughts. She's so authentically sweet I remind myself that I don't have anything to worry about. Besides, I have a daughter of my own who will one day be a young woman, and I would never want her to have to go through the injustices of unfounded judgement.

"You're too kind," I offer. "Would you like to see your room?"

Holly's eyes light up. "I'd love that."

I escort her upstairs, giving her an official tour while Rick stays with Lissa in the lounge. I notice the new nanny's eyes roaming across the family pictures on the wall. Scrutinizing would be a better word. She leans close until she's an inch or two from the frame. I'm taken aback for a second. It seems out of character for her to be so nosy.

"Sorry," she says, noticing me watching. "I love family photos." She blushes, and I decide not to say anything. Though it does strike me as slightly odd. Surely anything more than a quick glance is a little intrusive.

We come to the end of the hallway, and I open the last door on the left.

"This is the guest room, but feel free to make it your own and personalize it how you wish." I grin. "Within reason, of course. Maybe don't paint it black."

She laughs. "Don't worry. I won't. I left my Wednesday Addams cosplay at home." She slides across the room to the windows and looks down. "That's a great view of the backyard. I love all your hydrangea bushes."

"Gorgeous, aren't they?" I gesture to the floral arrangement of lavender and pale-blue hydrangeas brought in from the backyard. They're placed in a crystal vase in the center of the vanity drawers. A rectangular mirror hangs on the wall above it. "I had to bring some into the house. I figured they would tie in well with the room."

"Oh, wow. I can see why you opened a floral shop." She fingers a petal.

"I'd best leave you to settle in. There are brand-new clean sheets on your bed. New towels, too, also already run through the washer and dryer. You'll have your own attached bathroom, too, so you won't have to share with Jace."

Holly gives me an appreciative look. "Thank you for the hospitality. I'm feeling at home already."

"Excellent, as you should. If you need anything at all, just let us know."

Holly slowly spins to assess the room before her eyes land on me again. "It couldn't be more perfect."

The next morning, I stand in the bathroom and smudge a liquid blusher across my cheekbones. My fingers tremble slightly as I tut at myself for bringing the pink color too far down my face. It's my first day back at the floral shop since having Lissa. A million emotions are running rampant through my mind. It's such a bizarre process to leave your children in someone else's hands, even someone as qualified as Holly. And yet I'm entitled to have a life outside of being a mother. Juggling my passions, my career, and my duties as a mom is not going to be easy. I'm sure I'll be second-guessing myself the entire time. But on the flip side, Rick has never questioned his decision to go back to his sales job. Why should I worry about returning to my small business?

I'm not the only working mother in the world facing these types of challenges. I'm not the first to feel judged or to place impossible standards on myself. At the end of the day, Holly came with great credentials. The last family she worked with provided an amazing reference. It's time to stop being so hard on myself.

Lissa begins to cry. Despite having Holly in the house, it's second nature for me to go to her. I place the blusher stick down then notice how Lissa's wails taper to a soft whimper before dissolving completely.

Her nursery door is ajar when I reach it. Holly has gotten to her first. Settling into her role nicely, Holly coos to my baby girl as she whisks her across the room to the changing table and sets her down, offering her a crinkle toy to play with while she changes the dirty diaper.

Lissa starts babbling and shoves the toy into her mouth, gumming and gnawing at it.

"Good morning," I say and sidle over to them.

Holly whips around, fresh-faced and smiley. Her hair is pulled up in a ponytail without a single strand out of place. "Good morning."

I lean down and plant a kiss on Lissa's soft forehead. "And good morning to you, baby doll."

"Sorry. I heard her crying, and I just figured you were busy getting ready."

"You don't have to apologize for doing your job," I tell her.

Holly expertly straps on a new diaper and scoops Lissa up from the changing pad. "All better!"

"Mom, have you seen my math book?" Jace stands in the doorway, groggy-eyed, leaning his shoulder against the doorframe as if it's the only thing holding him upright.

"Sweetie, how many times do I have to tell you that you need to be more responsible—"

"I saw it in the game room last night," Holly cuts in, her eyes panning between me and Jace as if she's worried about overstepping an invisible boundary.

"Oh, see? Now say thank you to Holly." I raise my eyebrows at him, making it clear he has to do what I say.

"Thank you," Jace mumbles. He pushes himself off the doorframe and heads toward the game room.

The Nanny's Secret

Holly turns to me. "I saw him in there playing a video game last night. He had the math book with him."

I swallow the thought that it's so strange having someone in our house moving around noticing what we're doing. Of course Holly is allowed to explore. It's not like she stepped into Rick's and my bedroom.

"Thanks for letting me know," I say, hearing the slight edge to my voice. "Jace is not allowed to play Rick's video games. If you see him doing that again, please redirect him to something else and remind him that he shouldn't be doing that. He knows better, but he might try to make you think otherwise."

"Oh, of course. No problem." Her eyes flash before they flick down to Lissa. "Thanks for the clarification."

Worried I sounded bossy, I give her arm a gentle squeeze. "You didn't know. We're flexible. We don't expect you to immediately be acclimated. Getting to know us will take time. That works both ways, of course."

Holly nods, lifting her gaze back to me. "Absolutely. Do you want me to take Jace to school?"

I glance at my watch. "That would be wonderful. I really need to finish getting ready."

Rick leaves early and is already on his way to his office downtown, where he works as a sales manager. He puts in lots of hours, always seeking a way to get promoted. It's admirable, but having him gone so often is why I need Holly.

"No problem. I'll just get her dressed." She hugs Lissa closely and nuzzles their noses together. "Isn't that right, cutie pie?"

Lissa babbles happily.

I'm relieved Lissa is taking so well to Holly—and so quickly. Which is a good thing, I remind myself. I want Lissa to love the nanny. I just don't want to feel replaced.

"Can I have a quick cuddle before I leave?" I ask.

"Of course!"

Gently, Holly transfers Lissa to me. I breathe in the baby scent and hold her close to my body. The sudden prickle of tears takes me by surprise.

"Wow, this is harder than I thought." I pass her back before I lose my nerve.

"She's going to be just fine," Holly says. "Go and enjoy your first day at work."

I nod. She's right. I'm being ridiculous.

Downstairs I grab my purse and keys and shuffle to the pantry, giving Holly a rundown of what to feed Lissa during the day, since she's still being introduced to solid foods. We are trying to be careful to make sure she doesn't have any allergies. Holly promises to specifically stick to the jars of baby food I point out.

I pluck a banana from the basket on the counter and start to peel it. "Don't let Jace eat too much junk food when he gets home from school. He comes home ravenous every day, like he hasn't had a meal in weeks."

Holly laughs. "I get it. He's a growing boy. I'll keep an eye on it."

"Thank you."

I give Lissa a kiss, attempting to peck one on Jace's cheek, too, when he shuffles down the stairs, but he squirms out of my grasp. I wave goodbye to everybody as we file out

The Nanny's Secret

of the house together, me to my car, Jace and the baby going with Holly to hers.

I watch as Holly diligently straps Lissa into her car seat and Jace shoves his math book into his book bag, zipping it closed.

"Remember your seat belt," I call out to him, and he responds with an eye roll.

"Have a great day, everyone." I look at Holly with what I hope is warmth and confidence in my eyes as I say, "And good luck."

She nods back, a knowing smile playing at her lips. I turn away and get into my own car. Then I glance back at Holly. She isn't smiling anymore. Instead she's focused on reversing out of the drive.

Chapter 3

When I walk in the back door of my floral shop, Blossoms and Bouquets, my assistant, Serena, is already behind the counter, head bent over purchase orders. Her cherry-red lips pucker into a grin when she sees me enter.

Lilies and roses cloud the air with perfume. I gently plump up a display near the door and smile at the cut flowers kept in staggered bins by the wall. We have a few hanging baskets trailing down from the ceiling. Blossoms and Bouquets is spelled out in a large neon sign hanging on the wall, near a display of vases and bell bars on a shelf. Garlands of dried wildflowers hang down in bunches around the sign and the shelves. I breathe it all in, smiling to myself. It's good to be back.

"Hey, Audrey!"

Serena is twenty-seven and has a degree in floral design and marketing. She's my right-hand woman who kept everything ticking over nicely while I took my mater-

The Nanny's Secret

nity leave. She's done a wonderful job of holding down the fort, and as much as I hate to admit it, she could probably run things smoothly without me in the picture at all. However, I love my job and spent my savings on this dream. I'm lucky to have Serena to run things, but I'm lucky to be here too.

"Hi." I dip into my office, which is barely more than the size of a closet, to put my purse down. Then I sweep into the main sales floor, joining her at the register behind the counter. Today is all about catching up. I need Serena to tell me how our orders are going and what we'll be working on for the next few weeks.

And truth be told, I'm nervous. I'm not sure if I'm even going to be able to jump straight back in. But here I am, on the diving board. Maybe not the high one, but the baby one for now.

"Welcome back, boss! How are you feeling this morning?" she asks. She tucks a curl behind her ear.

"Lots of emotions," I admit, trying to contain the tears waiting to bloom behind my eyes.

"You're going to do great," she says, giving my arm a squeeze.

"I hope you're right." I focus on the papers spread out in front of her. "How are things looking?"

"Oh." Serena shakes her head, as if to clear it and bring herself back to focus. "I'm just going through the current orders." She picks up a stack and taps them on the glass counter to arrange them neatly.

"Wow." My eyes go large. "That many, huh?"

"Yep," Serena says. "You were right about that wedding

fair. It really drummed up new business. But I guess we can't complain about having too much work to do."

"Indeed not," I agree, scanning through the orders briefly.

"This order is the biggest, so I put it in the front." Serena slides the paper over to me.

"A bridal bouquet with red and white roses. Excellent."

"I can help you get started on that," Serena offers.

"Sounds good. Let me just look through the rest of these real fast."

I mill through the stack, putting the orders due last at the bottom, noticing that Serena has already placed the more pressing ones toward the top.

Serena and I head toward the back of the sales floor to the workshop. We have a view of the entire store and the door leading in. If a customer comes in needing assistance, we can be there in a breeze and be able to take note of anything going on. The building I rent is small, but the space is manageable and well equipped for Serena and me to be able to multitask.

After a while, I head to the back to check my phone and get a drink of water. The temptation to call home is strong. Perhaps just a quick check-in. Holly answers on the first ring, and I'm relieved when I hear Lissa cackling in the background.

"We've just had a morning walk in the stroller. Lissa was squealing at all the birds," Holly says. Her voice is as sweet as honeysuckle.

"She loves pigeons," I say. "So everything's okay?"

"Oh, yes. It's all going extremely well. I don't want you

to worry about us while you're at work, Audrey. We're having a blast here."

"I'm happy to hear it. I sure do miss Lissa, but I'm glad she's having fun with you."

After Holly and I sort out a few other things in the kids' schedules, I return to the workshop, walking with a lighter step. Maybe I worried for nothing. This whole thing is a breeze. I can be a working mom and not fall apart after all.

However, by lunch, when I come up for air again, I'm second-guessing that short-lived optimism. I have a missed call from Rick, which is unusual. He never calls me from work. There's also a long list of notifications lighting up my screen. I hadn't realized I'd put my phone on silent, a rookie mistake for a new mom with a baby and a nanny at home.

Before diving into the swarm, I step into my office and call Rick first.

"Have you been on social media?" he asks as soon as he answers.

His clipped tone briefly startles me, and I manage a strained chuckle. "Well... hello to you too."

"Audrey, this is important." His voice holds no amusement, sucking the marrow from my bones.

"Which platform?" I ask.

"All of them," he replies. "Your name and picture are all the rage right now, with an emphasis on the rage part."

"Seriously?"

"Yes," he says. "I don't know what the hell is going on, Audrey."

"Neither do I, Rick. I'm not exactly present on social media. You know I don't understand that stuff." I pull in a deep breath. "Okay. Do you want to tell me what it's about before I look myself? Just so I'll be prepared?"

"It's not good." Rick's voice is flat and emotionless. He sounds like that when he's very angry, and that doesn't happen often. "There is a picture of you floating around that's gone viral. It looks like it originated on Twitter, although I am having trouble identifying the original source. People are going crazy about it."

"What kind of picture, Rick?" The frustration sounds in my raised voice. Why won't he say?

"You have this twisted smile on your face, and you're stepping on a cat's tail. The cat looks like it's in pain."

"A— What? A— *Cat's* tail? We don't even own a cat."

His sigh bursts through the phone speaker, and he sounds tired. "Yeah, I'm aware of that, Audrey."

"Well then, where did it come from?"

"I don't know. Hang on." I hear crackles over the phone as if he's putting his hand over the receiver. I hear him talking to a muffled voice in the background. He comes back clear again a second later. "I have to go. Work meeting. Just... just check it out for yourself."

"Okay, bye then."

He hangs up. My hands are shaking. Does he think this picture is real? Is he mad at me or the situation?

I'm trembling as I click through the notifications on my phone until I find it. Plain as day, as sharp as the blue sky above, is a picture of me. It's undeniably me. In the picture, I'm standing on a cat's tail, and I look like I'm having a good time doing it. I'm smiling wide, a look of pure joy on my face. I can't tell when or where the real

The Nanny's Secret

picture was taken, but I don't look much younger than I am now.

The image has obviously been doctored. I've never stepped on a cat. Ever. But whoever did this has done a good job. It looks like a screen grab from a security camera or doorbell. It's grainy. I'm on the front porch of a house I don't recognize, and I'm looking directly at the camera with a huge smile on my face. A front yard is behind me, leading to a road. But aside from that there are no defining features. It looks like any old porch on any old street.

Someone has found a picture of me online, possibly from the website for Blossoms and Bouquets or one of my old social media pictures, and they've added my face to this monstrosity. And then they uploaded it onto the Internet to hurt me.

Bile rises from the pit of my stomach as I go through the notifications on my phone. I scroll past the names of my friends and family. People I went to school with. A cousin we've invited over at the holidays a couple times.

Audrey, what's going on? Audrey, did you step on a cat's tail? Why? Audrey, what did you do to that poor creature? It's sick.

Then there are the tweets and Facebook posts about me that are so cripplingly vicious that I know I'll be haunted by them for a long time.

Audrey Miller, florist by day, animal abuser by night.

Why does that shop Blossoms and Bouquets support animal cruelty?

Support local! As long as it's not Blossoms and Bouquets! Stay the hell away from them!

Audrey Miller needs to be in jail.

Audrey Miller is a sick, sick person and should be strung up!

The room is spinning. I would never intentionally hurt an animal. I don't even kill spiders when I see them in my house. I wait for them to crawl onto a paper towel, and then I put them outside.

I don't even have a cat, nor do I recognize the one in the photo with me. It's a short-haired cat with tan and white stripes going through its middle and down its clamped tail. Its mouth is open in visible pain. I have no idea if this cat is even real. It certainly looks like it. The photoshop quality is so expertly done that unless you are me and know it's fake, it's impossible to tell that it's not a real picture. I feel sorry for this poor creature being treated in this way.

Gutted, I drag my back against the wall and sink to the floor, tucking my knees up to my chin. Underneath the picture are a slew of death threats from people I don't even know. I swallow down the nausea churning in my stomach and place my forehead on my knees, forcing myself to breathe in, breathe out. There has to be an explanation for this. I'm going to figure it out. I'm going to fix this.

My reputation, and my career, both depend on it.

Chapter 4
HOLLY

I stand in the center of the bedroom, looking for a place to start. My gaze sweeps across the bed, then the armoire in the corner, and finally curves across to the dresser on the other side of the room. And that's not all. There are the bedside tables too.

If I'm going to find what I want, I need to get a move on. Chewing the inside of my cheek, I hurry over to the first bedside table. It's time for secrets to reveal themselves. Before I start, I check the baby monitor in my hand. The screen is tiny, but Lissa is there, lying sprawled out like a starfish in her crib, chest rising and falling peacefully as she naps. Good.

The wood groans as I pull it open. Despite appearances, much of the fancy furniture in this room is in fact cheap and badly made. I yank the drawer of the bedside table open the last inch, rifle through the annoyingly humdrum contents—ear plugs, sleep masks, a box of antacids and a retainer—then move on to the next table.

There lies a book, a little package of tissues, and a charger for an electronic device. Nothing incriminating.

The next drawer contains contact solution, a self-help book—it's so ironic, I laugh—and an iPad. Nothing else. Not even a vibrator or any sort of sex toy. Unless those are hidden somewhere else. Not that I'm looking for that. No, I have more important items to unearth here.

Next the dresser. I quickly flit through underwear and T-shirts and towels. After I push the last drawer closed, I linger on the photograph of *him* that's sitting on top of the storage unit. In the picture, he's smiling, dashing, handsome. My eyes narrow, and I tilt my head to the side, studying him. My finger brushes lightly across his chest in the photo. He's wearing a pine-green, short-sleeved polo shirt.

I recoil as if touching the image of him will burn my skin.

Come on, Holly. It's only a matter of time.

I just need to be patient. Vigilant. I'll keep looking. I know I'll find what I'm looking for. I just have to stay calm and careful.

I glance at the baby monitor. Lissa is starting to stir, her eyelids fluttering, little knees bending up. I scurry out of the room, the monitor in my hand, and seal the door shut just the way it was, leaving no trace I'd been there at all.

Chapter 5

I open the door to a quiet house. Walking on tired legs, I make my way through the house and find Holly in the backyard with Lissa. Then I remember Jace is at baseball practice. Rick is still at work for at least another hour. I should go outside and let Holly know I'm here, maybe spend some quality time with Lissa, but I can't bring myself to do it. I don't want to paint on a sunny disposition. Not when nothing but storm clouds are roiling inside me.

After finding the photoshopped image of me and the poor cat, I spent the rest of the working day in a daze. Serena offered to take me out to lunch to keep my mind off the whole ordeal, but I didn't want to show my face anywhere. Even when Serena pointed out that I hadn't done anything wrong, I couldn't shake the feeling of it. I suspect even a long, scalding shower won't scrub the dirt of it away.

But I also refused to leave the shop early. I stayed the entire day. Now that I'm home, I pour myself a glass of merlot and plop down on the couch with a long sigh, feeling like my mind weighs a million pounds. I see Holly and Lissa through the living room window. My baby girl giggles as Holly pushes her gently on the swing. Lissa's short blond hair flutters upward in the breeze. Her gray eyes are pointed at the sky, watching the patches of white fluffy clouds roll through.

I love her, my beautiful miracle rainbow baby. She came along just as I was starting to give up hope that I would ever be able to conceive again. It had been a long journey of tests and trials at fertility clinics, but there she is.

Jace will always be my first, my boy, and I love him with all my heart. Lissa is hope made flesh. The light of my life. It occurs to me then that Jace might end up seeing the photo. His Internet usage is still restricted by Rick and me, but I'm not stupid. I know even preteens end up seeing awful things. I bite my lip, hoping I won't have to explain it to him. The thought of sitting him down and telling him all about this photo makes my chest feel tight.

Instead, I look at Holly, her youthful figure, the sleek curve of her hips, the dip in her lower back. Recently, I've been telling myself that I don't need to hit the gym and lose the baby weight. It's perfectly fine to carry a few extra pounds. But here I am, comparing myself to a younger model. No, I refuse to let myself do that. Holly is here for me. To help me.

But as soon as she turned up, my life was thrown into turmoil. Is it a coincidence that the fake photo went viral on her first day? Or is it more than that? I play back our

The Nanny's Secret

conversations but can't place anything specific that would make her want to ruin me like that.

There was the issue with Jace and the video games, but I wasn't exactly reprimanding her. Well, not the way I saw it. Maybe Holly assumed or heard it differently. I thought I'd been firm but polite about asking her not to let Jace play those games. Could she really be that upset and hold that much of a grudge? Surely not. I hadn't been that harsh with her. She didn't seem upset at the time. Unless I failed to see the warning signs.

I sip the merlot and mentally run through every single person I know. From my family to Rick's family, to old customers who complained about an order, to friends I lost touch with over the years. My mind sweeps through potential enemies like I'm flicking through an old rolodex. There was one kid at Jace's school who got into a fight with Jace. The parents asked the school to suspend him even though both boys were at fault. I remember the hard-faced father and pinch-mouthed mother. Perhaps they did it.

Then I gaze out of the window to the house across the street. To Emma and Elijah's house. I shake my head slightly and pull my eyes away.

After another swig of merlot, I swipe my phone screen to wake it and cringe at the nasty image. It's such a strange thing to do. Then I pull up the search engine bar, trying to find the original source of that image.

I'm so immersed in the rabbit hole that I startle when the back door slams. I nearly spill my wine on my shirt, glancing up to see Holly and Lissa coming back inside.

"Oh, hi, Holly. Sorry, I was going to come outside and

greet you two. It's just—"

"No problem," she says. Then her eyes narrow slightly. She must be taking in the sight of me on the sofa, eyes red from crying, the half-empty glass of wine. "Are you all right?"

"Well, I..." I trail off, suddenly self-conscious. I'm sure my appearance is somewhat haggard after the day I've had.

"Oh no. Did you have a bad first day back?" Her eyebrows bunch up in concern, and for a moment I'm not sure if she's mocking me.

I try to scoff, but it comes out sounding more anguished, like a croak. "That's putting it lightly."

Holly lifts Lissa and sits down next to me on the couch. Lissa reaches out to me, and I place her in my lap, kissing the top of her head.

"Ba-ba-ba," Lissa babbles.

"I missed you today," I whisper into the curve of her soft ear.

"She's been the perfect baby all day," Holly says with a smile.

"Good," I murmur.

She nods. "So tell me all about your day. It can't have been that bad."

"You mean you haven't heard all about it?" I ask. "I've gone viral."

If Holly is pretending to be innocent, as her expression reflects, I see no sign of acting or amusement to prove it.

"Viral?"

My shoulders wilt into the cushions behind me, and I let out a groan of angst. "Someone posted a horrible photo-

The Nanny's Secret

shopped picture of me on Twitter, and it's blown up. It's all over every social media platform."

"What kind of picture?"

"A picture of me stepping on a cat's tail."

"What?" she says. "That's so weird."

I burst out, "It's not real. I'm not an animal abuser."

"Of course you're not, Audrey. Why would anyone do that to you?"

I shake my head. "I have no idea."

"Did they mention you by name?"

I nod. "And they hit my business name too. People were writing such hateful comments. Sending me death threats. There are calls to boycott my shop."

"Oh, that's awful." She places a hand on her mouth for a moment. "Can I see the picture?"

I study her. Is it odd that she has no idea what's going on? "How do you not know about it already? It's gone viral."

Holly casts me an innocent shrug. "I've been busy with the baby all day. I don't have any social media accounts."

Suddenly, I remember this. She's telling the truth. I tried to look her up, before her interview, and couldn't find anything about her.

Holly clamps her hand over my shoulder. Her touch is tender, authentic. "It can't be so bad, can it? Not everyone uses social media, myself included. I just don't play into that fake hype that everybody posts about their perfect lives. Nobody's lives are 'perfect.'" She puts the word perfect into air quotations. "You're great with people and have a bubbly personality. I'm sure that anyone who comes into your shop or uses your business for their floral needs can see that."

"If I'll even have any customers after this." I sigh. "Damn. I guess I need to make a statement. Or maybe I shouldn't be acknowledging anything at all." I run my hands through my hair. There's no blueprint for dealing with something like this. I'm a floral shop owner, not a celebrity. I don't have a PR company telling me what to do.

Holly frowns, glancing down at my phone. "Let me see the picture."

Reluctantly, I pull it up. She examines it with a poker face, as if she's appraising an expensive piece of jewelry.

After a lingering moment, she offers my phone back. "It's a good photoshopping job."

My stomach knots. "A little too convincing."

"Can you track down the original source?"

"I don't know. I hope so. I'm trying to do that now, but to be honest I don't really know where to start," I say.

Holly reaches her hand out to take my phone again, her eyebrows arching. "May I?"

I shrug and hand it over. "Be my guest. I'm hitting dead ends left and right."

"Maybe there's a way to track down the original image by searching for it a certain way." Holly sets to work, and I watch her diligently as she types out certain phrasing and scrolls through images of similar content.

"Hmm. We might be getting somewhere." Holly's eyes scan the screen with undeniable concentration. I have to admit, I admire her dedication to the cause. If she's willing to dig this deep to help me out, then I can't possibly think

The Nanny's Secret

she's involved somehow. Unless that's what she wants me to believe. I feel guilty even entertaining the idea. I enlisted her to watch my baby. I need to trust her.

Holly's shoulders straighten in surprise. "Huh. Well, that's— interesting."

"What is it?" I can hardly hear my own voice over the rushing sound of my heartbeat hammering through my ears.

"It looks like this image was used from a clip of a small, independent movie." Holly turns the phone screen toward me. "Right here. Look. It's the same."

And there it is. The original image in all its glory. The shoe and the cat and the background matches perfectly. But someone else's face is on the body of the woman.

My fingers travel across my mouth. "Oh my God!"

Holly nods conspiratorially, meeting my gaze. "Crazy."

"This is so random. I've never been the victim of a social defamation like this."

"At least you have the proof now," she says. "Maybe you can contact some of the social media apps and ask them to take it down."

It seems like a long shot. Speaking to a lawyer wouldn't hurt either. My thoughts are racing as Lissa reaches for the remote beside me on the end table. She tries to shove it into her mouth, but Holly is faster, offering her a toy instead.

"Smooth." I laugh and stroke Lissa's fine hair.

Holly gives me the humble smile of someone who is just trying to do something she's naturally good at. "Thanks."

"Can I check something?" I gesture for the laptop.

Holly passes it over, and I browse through the website for Blossoms and Bouquets. A photograph of me is on the website, and I want to see if it matches the face in the viral photo. But my face has been altered so much on the fake picture that it's hard to tell. Then I quickly scroll through the business Instagram account, along with my private one.

"I thought if I knew where the person got the picture of me, I might be able to narrow down who it was," I say. "Some of my photos are private. But they've put it through so many filters, it's hard to tell." I sigh. "Okay, so what should I do next? I hate to ask because you've helped me so much already."

Holly looks up from her phone. "So, I'm reading the Wikipedia page for the movie. It was a stunt, apparently, and the cat wasn't harmed. It just looks that way."

I bounce Lissa on my lap. "Well, that's a relief."

"Just upload the original, non-photoshopped picture with the caption from the movie set. It will prove it's not you." She shrugs. "It won't fix everything. It probably won't go as viral as the original. But you have something to prove you didn't do it. Which is great!"

I thank her and busy myself screenshotting the picture. Then I post it to my social media platforms, along with an explanation and paragraphs from the Wikipedia page. Holly takes Lissa upstairs to change her diaper, and I wait for the reactions to the new post to come in. In fifteen minutes, I receive one comment. As I feared, the damage is already done. Most people are going to continue to think I'm a terrible person. But why would someone target me like this?

Chapter 6

As I turn down the side street in front of the floral shop, I notice Serena crouched on the pavement outside. A white bucket is beside her. She pushes her hand into the bucket and brings out an industrial-sized sponge, wrings it, and wipes the door.

I slow down and pull up to the curb, rolling down the window in front of her.

Serena turns around, wiping her hands on a blue bandana.

"Audrey!" A fixed grin freezes her features. "Please don't freak out."

"What happened?" My eyes scan over the red paint graffiti running across the front of my store.

Serena has already tried her best to scrub most of it away, but I can still see where the letters had formed the words Animal Hater. The red paint bleeds down the glass, fading to a foamy pink.

"I found it here when I arrived." Serena winces as if she thinks I'll find her personally responsible.

Humiliation turns my cheeks vermillion.

"It's all right. Just... just go inside," I say. Sweat beads on my forehead. I can barely look at the graffiti across the shop. "You don't need to clean this up. It'll take you all day. I'll call somebody out here to fix this. A professional."

"Are you sure?" She slowly stands and drops the sponge into the water.

"Yes. And thank you for trying." Tears burn behind my eyes. I try not to let them show as I roll the car toward the back parking lot.

By the time I've parked the car, my hands are shaking uncontrollably. But I'm determined not to cry. This person doesn't deserve my tears, so I clear my throat and lift my chin.

Last night, when Rick came home, we discussed the photoshopped picture and who might have done it. He thinks it's a disgruntled customer, but with me being on maternity leave, it seems a little odd. Serena is the person the customers have seen for the last six months. My face is on the website, but I haven't been in the shop for a long time. Then there's figuring out which photo was used. Could it be one I've shared on social media? Or a private photo? It's hard to tell. If it is a private photo, then I know someone close to me did this. If it's a photo grabbed from my website, then it could be anyone.

Before setting foot inside the shop, I grab my phone and call Rick. It's only when he answers that the unshed tears come thick and fast.

The Nanny's Secret

"Honey, what's wrong?" he asks, urgency in his voice. "Is it the kids?"

"No," I say, pulling myself together. "No, the kids are fine. It's the floral shop. Someone has defaced it."

"What do you mean defaced?" he asks.

"They spray painted Animal Hater across the door and window. God, Rick, it's such a mess." I wipe a sheen of sweat from my forehead.

"Shit," he says. "Is this going to slow down business? Because if the floral shop stops making money, we need to have some serious conversations."

His words give me pause. His first concern is *money*? I'm so shocked I don't say anything for a few seconds.

"Audrey?" he prompts.

"Would you buy flowers from an animal hater?" I ask, the words coming through my teeth.

He lets out a sharp breath. "I need to get back to work."

"Yeah, me too," I say. "Thanks for asking how I am."

He sighs. "I'm sorry. Are you all right?"

"I'm fine." I hang up as soon as the words are out of my mouth.

Serena emerges from the back door as I'm putting the phone back in my pocket.

"I called a cleaning company," she calls out.

"Thanks. I really appreciate it." I don't tell her that I'm now concerned about how much the cleanup is going to cost, thanks to Rick reminding me we can barely afford to run the shop.

Serena studies me. "Are you okay?"

"About as well as can be expected." I try to smile but

suspect it comes across as forced. "Right, I'm going to have a quick cup of coffee in my office and try not to think about all this nonsense."

"Good," she says. "I'll see you in ten."

Serena heads off to the workshop to start a new flower arrangement, and I flop down in my office chair. I turn on my computer, but I can't focus on any of the work in front of me. I try to think of who would have targeted me and why.

My brain keeps circling back to Holly.

Holly.

Holly.

Holly.

The name thrums through my brain and ricochets across my scalp. Why do my gut instincts keep careening back to her?

I'm a good person. Well, at least I try to be. I don't have any enemies. I've never so much as gotten into an altercation with a stranger at a store or at a traffic light. Why would anyone come at my jugular like this?

It just doesn't make any sense. None of these horrible things started happening to me until Holly entered the picture. I prop my elbows up on my desk and scrub a hand over my face.

Also, she was so fast at locating the original source of that picture on the Internet. How could she have found it so quickly? That low-budget film might not have even seen the light of day, much less have been popular. For someone who claims to not have an online presence, she sure knew

The Nanny's Secret

how to type in all the right things into the search bar to pull up that video still.

Something isn't adding up, and it's leaving a sour taste in my mouth. An unsettled sensation bubbles in my stomach, like acid rising and spreading through my veins.

The phone rings. I cringe and recoil on myself like a crushed soda can when Serena answers, and I hear her apologizing and trying to be diplomatic as a customer cancels an order. This is a nightmare. I'll have to call the police too. We have a security camera at the front of the shop. Perhaps it picked up a good view of the vandal.

I scan my email inbox, finding three more cancellations and a demand for a refund. This could put me out of business at this rate. My body turns hot with rage, and I decide to do something proactive. I search through the darkest archives of my memories. Through all my secrets. One screams at me, but I'm not sure I'm ready to face it. Paranoia is a dark current ready to sweep me under. I remind myself not to unearth what needs to remain hidden. There's a reason they are locked in the vault. That's where they need to stay, forever. The ramifications will inflict too much damage, and I'm not ready to face those consequences.

Chapter 7

I decide to call the police and officially record the graffiti, the death threats, and the doctored photo. At least with everything made official, we can go through the insurance company to pay for the store cleanup. The officer tells me to begin documenting everything. I take screenshots of insults. Then I make a file in my folder just for harassment.

The rest of the day goes by in a blur. We have several cancellations, including a huge order for a wedding. I can already see the income dropping, and with each dollar lost, my stomach squirms.

But life goes on, and not long after locking up the shop, I'm home, serving up dinner for the family. Jace sits down at the dinner table and plants both his elbows on the surface. He's got a fork in one hand, a knife in the other. No one has managed to sit at a table with so much attitude.

"Where's Holly?" he demands.

"She has the night off." I place my napkin in my lap

The Nanny's Secret

and nudge my chin at his arms. "Elbows off the table, please."

Since the photo went viral, I've been careful around Jace, searching for signs that he might have seen the doctored image. But so far he seems completely oblivious to it.

Jace groans and leans back in his chair. He starts twirling his spaghetti around on his fork until there is a huge mound of it, but he doesn't bring it to his mouth. Instead, his eyes lift to me then to Rick.

Rick and I have been quiet with each other since the phone conversation. He hasn't apologized for being insensitive, and I haven't apologized for hanging up on him. I half expected him to ask for an update on the shop's finances when I came home.

"Will she be back later?" Jace asks.

"Who?" I ask, spaced out by the rush of thoughts running through my head.

Jace rolls his eyes. "Holly."

"Oh. Well, yeah. She lives here, Jacey. She needs to come back in order to sleep." I smile at my son.

"Right." Jace doesn't hide a smile and brings the forkful of noodles to his mouth. "She's funny. And she likes baseball. She promised to come to one of my practices soon."

I exchange a curious look with Rick, whose eyebrows are arched so high they are starting to disappear behind his hairline.

"You like the new nanny, buddy?" Rick asks, slathering butter across his bread roll.

Jace blushes and scratches the side of his cheek. "She's cool, I guess."

Rick smirks at me. I'm confused for a moment, given the tense atmosphere between us, but then I know what the look insinuates. Rick thinks Jace has a crush on Holly. And now that I think about it, he's right. Jace seems taken with Holly, and I'm not sure how I feel about that. I need to keep an eye on him. He's only twelve, and these preteen years are very impressionable.

Rick leans back, stretching before taking a sip of water. "Well, I for one think it's great you've taken such a quick liking to Holly."

Jace's gaze rises from his plate. "You do?"

"Of course. I want to feel comfortable with the person watching my kids, especially if they're living in our house," he adds.

"Will she live with us forever?" Jace's eyes brighten.

"Well." I release a soft chuckle that I hope sounds breezy. "I don't know if she'll live with us forever, but for the indefinite future, yes, probably."

"Isn't the indefinite future and forever one and the same?" Rick asks in a teasing voice.

I give him a look, and his amused smile turns into stoicism as he finally picks up that I want him to do some parenting rather than amuse himself.

"Anyway, Jace, I'm glad you like Holly, but she's your nanny. Okay, bud? Not a friend or anything like that." Rick turns to me, and his eyebrows rise as if to silently say, "There, is that better?"

"I agree wholeheartedly with everything your father

just said." I pat Rick's hand. I hope the words get through to Jace. I'm still not sure how I feel about Holly, especially when Jace is so enamored with her.

Jace props one elbow up on the table and leans his head against his hand, pushing the spaghetti around on his plate. "Whatever."

"We're not saying that you can't have fun," I add, enjoying being good cop today. "Just don't make her feel overwhelmed. Okay, honey?"

Beside me, Lissa bangs her spoon against the side of her high chair tray. Little noodle flecks are in her hair, and her entire face is stained orange from the sauce. She squeals with delight and shovels in another handful of noodles that I've processed to help her nosh on them more easily.

As we're clearing the table a few minutes later, Holly returns home. Jace is soon on her heels, talking her ear off about his day. I frown, mentally acknowledging the fact that he's never once shown that kind of enthusiasm to me about school. And he clearly hasn't understood what we were trying to say to him.

Rick greets her with a high-five and asks how her dinner out with friends went. I'm in the background, like a wallflower, listening to the conversation and feeling like I'm being phased out.

Nonetheless, I breeze into the kitchen with a stack of plates, stitching on my most sincere smile as I say to Holly, "Welcome home! I hope you had a lovely evening."

She turns around, but her eyes scroll me up and down before she breaks into her own smile, as if I'm the stranger and she's the one who belongs here. At least that's how it feels. I'm on edge from all the negativity lately. I don't need to project my frustration and suspicions on Holly. She deserves better. And so do my children, whom I've put in Holly's care.

Holly's gaze passes over my shoulder to Lissa, who is still cackling to herself and banging her spoon against the tray.

"She's a mess. I'll take her up for her bath now while you guys finish up in here," Holly says.

"Thanks—" I start.

"Wait, I'm coming with you," Jace interrupts, almost barreling over me in the process to get to Holly.

"Homework time, buddy," I tell him.

Jace glances at Holly as if he's hoping she might save him, but she shrugs. "Sorry, if your mom says do your homework, then you need to do your homework."

I give her a thankful smile, grateful for the small victory.

Holly scoops a babbling Lissa from her seat and starts trotting with her up the stairs, with Jace on her heels and Lissa giving her a doe-eyed gaze of affection.

"Everything all right?"

I startle as Rick comes up behind me. His arms rub up and down my arms. "Are you still mad at me?"

"I don't know," I say honestly.

"Honey, I hope you realize you have my full support. And now you have Holly living here, helping us out." He wraps his arms around me and squeezes tight. "Just try not to worry too much."

"How am I supposed to do that when you're so both-

The Nanny's Secret

ered by how much the shop is making?" I ask. "And I still want to find out who did this to me, Rick. I called the police today. I've started documenting everything."

He steps away. "I think that's a good idea. I would too."

I purse my lips. It all feels too little too late. I love my husband, but he didn't exactly jump to my defense from the start.

"Come on, let's tag team this mess," I say, gesturing to the kitchen.

"You wash, and I'll dry? Just like we would do while we blasted records and sang at the tops of our lungs when we first moved in together in the city?" Rick cocks an eyebrow, some of that mischievousness lighting his eyes, a quality that attracted me to him so long ago. Rick is a good flirt. Too good.

I swat him with the dish rag. "I know what you're doing."

He puffs out his chest. "Oh yeah, what's that?"

"You're trying to butter me up."

"What's so wrong about that?"

I smirk at him, swatting him one more time with the towel before I turn to the sink. "Nothing, I suppose."

But secretly I'm still relaying all my fears that whirl around my mind. The photograph, the tension between Holly and me. The defaced store and the unhappy customers. The secrets I can't tell anyone. The way my son looks at the nanny with adoration. Suddenly, it all sounds like a recipe for a complete and utter disaster.

Chapter 8

The Saturday foot traffic at Blossoms and Bouquets is down. Serena notices it, too, and I can tell she's trying to keep me feeling positive as I busy myself with an online order.

We've had the graffiti professionally cleaned away. The store is looking pristine. I even added a promotion outside the store on two-for-one posies. And still the morning goes by slowly. After gobbling down a quick sandwich and a Sprite at lunch, I check my phone to see whether Holly or Rick will be bringing Jace to the store to help out for a little while.

Jace comes to the shop to do a bit of light cleaning for me at least two Saturdays a month. He usually enjoys it, especially since I pay him. It's a win-win situation. Jace learns life skills and gets some spending money, while I end up with a tidy shop. He's a surprisingly hard worker. And he's usually a few minutes early. Which is why I'm concerned when I

The Nanny's Secret

notice the time. I told Jace that I'd like him to be dropped off at around twelve-thirty so he has time to eat lunch first. The stock room needs organizing, and I have a load of scrap trash I need him to haul to the dumpsters behind the building.

Yet when I check my phone, it's almost one o'clock. There aren't any messages either. Jace can be moody at times, but if there was traffic, he would most likely drop me a text to let me know. I don't know who he was going to get to drop him off, so I dial Jace's number first, and it cuts straight to voice mail. Jace never turns his phone off either. He's attached to it, aside from when we take it at night when he's supposed to be in bed.

I call it again. Maybe the lines got crossed and he's trying to reach me. It cuts straight to voice mail the second time too.

My stomach tingles with anxiety. I call Rick next, and he answers on the second ring.

"Are you bringing Jace in to help me at the shop?"

"No. Why?"

I lean against the counter and blow out a frustrated breath. "He was supposed to be here a half hour ago."

"I'm sorry, babe. I'm at work."

"You went to the office today?"

"I had to," he says. "Peterson called me and asked me if I could put the finishing touches on this proposal for early next week."

It's not uncommon for Rick to put in longer hours, especially as he tries to climb the status rungs at his job. Sales and marketing take time and effort, I get that, but it doesn't help me now when I have to rule out the fact that our twelve-year-old son isn't currently with him.

"Was he home with Holly when you left for work?" I ask.

"Yeah, he was still sleeping," Rick says. "I left the house around ten."

"What were Holly and the baby doing when you left?"

"I think Holly was changing her diaper," Rick says.

I curse myself for not confirming plans with Holly or Rick about who would bring Jace to the shop. I just told Jace to be here by twelve-thirty, assuming he would be responsible enough to follow through. He's given me no reason not to trust him in the past about this kind of thing.

I sigh and rub my forehead. "All right. Well, Jace is not answering his cell phone."

"That's odd. Want me to try him?"

"If you don't mind. I'm going to call Holly. Let me know if you get a hold of either one of them."

"I did tell Holly to bring Jace into the store after lunch," Rick says. "She might have interpreted that to mean after one."

"That's true. What did she say back? Did she give you an indication of time?"

"No. She just said she'd bring him."

"Okay. Maybe they're running late." My heart calms slightly. "I think I should still call her, though, just to make sure. You try Jace. I'll call Holly, and we'll see if we get through."

"Sure," he says. "Try not to worry. Like you said, they're probably just running late."

The Nanny's Secret

"Yeah. I know. I just... With this graffiti and everything, I need to be sure."

"I get it, babe. Speak to you soon, okay?"

I hang up and dial Holly's number, but it also cuts to her voice mail. I'm so surprised she doesn't answer that it takes me a moment to find my voice. Pushing off the counter, I start pacing the showroom floor as I leave a message, trying not to sound frantic.

"Holly, it's Audrey. Jace was supposed to be at the shop half an hour ago. His phone is off. What's going on? Please call me as soon as you can."

My hands are starting to shake as I push the end call button. I keep pacing, unable to focus on anything, unable to calm the anxiety brewing in my chest. Did they get into an accident? It's too much of a coincidence that neither of them are answering their phones. It's ten minutes past one now. I wring my hands together, trying to remind myself that Holly probably doesn't know Jace was supposed to be here forty minutes ago.

Still, I don't like this. A few days ago, I opened my inbox to a barrage of death threats, and now my son is missing. Someone targeted me specifically with a nasty photoshop. What if they went after my son too? Dark thoughts build and build, pushing against the back of my skull, growing talons and ready to cut deep.

I call over to Serena to let her know I'm going out for a while, grab my purse, and jog to the front door. My thoughts race at a million miles an hour. Whoever is doing this has already won because I've played out every worst-case scenario on the way to the car. I picture Jace lying bruised and broken in a hospital bed. I hear Lissa's shrieking cry in my ears. I can't turn off these invasive thoughts. They hit me like bullets.

It takes thirty minutes to drive home, though it feels like two hours. Holly's car isn't in the driveway. I hastily park and head inside, rushing through every room, finding them empty. No one is in the house, no sign of them anywhere. I glance in the backyard. They aren't there either.

Next I drive down to the neighborhood park. Maybe they took a quick trip there and lost track of time. I'm sure there's an explanation. There has to be. Every time I hear a siren wailing in the distance, a pulse of panic ripples through my body.

It takes another fifteen minutes. Precious seconds that drag on like hours. Only one car is in the parking lot, and it's not Holly's. A man wearing a tan sweater pushes a little girl in pigtails on the swing. Otherwise, the park is empty. Now what? I head home and dial Rick's number again before I'm even through the garage door.

"They aren't at home or in the park," I say.

"I couldn't get through either," he admits. "I've tried a few times now."

"Our kids are in this woman's care, and she's not answering her phone—"

"All right, sweetie, just try to calm down. I'm sure there's an explanation." Rick's voice is consoling but not enough to put my mind at ease.

"Did Holly mention taking the baby anywhere when you left this morning?"

The Nanny's Secret

Rick is silent for a moment. "No."

I groan and throw up my arms. "Where the hell could they be?"

"I don't know." Rick's voice is quiet. He's anxious too. I can tell. It's now after two, and we haven't been able to contact either of them for well over an hour.

"I'm calling the police," I say.

"Wait, check her room. Maybe her phone is there. Check Jace's room. Maybe they forgot them. Maybe they forgot all about coming to the shop."

"What are the chances of that happening?" I snap. "I'm hanging up to call the police. If you don't want to worry about it, then don't."

Before Rick can respond, I hear the front door open. I'm standing in the living room, so I spin on my heel to face the foyer.

Jace stumbles into the house, howling with laughter. Holly is holding Lissa on her right hip. She's laughing too.

"Holly, you are *hilarious*." I've never seen Jace so vibrant, his eyes alight with amusement.

My chest rises and falls fast. My fists tighten into clenched balls at my sides. My jaw locks, teeth gritting together. I'm ready to snap like a rubber band.

"They just walked in the front door," I mutter into the phone and then hang up.

I charge toward the foyer like a bull ready to fight. Holly's excuse had better be worth it.

Chapter 9

"Give me the baby," I demand.

While Holly stands there open-mouthed, I snatch Lissa from her arms. Lissa starts to cry. I hug her close to my chest, rubbing her back and swaying with her to calm her, but she keeps roaring in my ear, her wails growing louder because she's feeding on my anxiety.

Holly blinks at me, looking stunned.

"Mom!" Jace shouts. "What are you doing?"

Seething, I save my wrath for Holly, icy glare in place. "What the *hell* were you thinking?"

Holly's mouth opens then clamps shut.

"Where were you? Why didn't you answer any of my calls? Why didn't you bring Jace to the floral shop?" I glance at Jace. "You didn't answer your phone either, Jace. I didn't know where you were. I was so worried about you."

Fat tears brim at the edges of Holly's eyes. Her cheeks and neck blotch a patchy red.

"I'm... sorry," she stammers.

The Nanny's Secret

"You're *sorry?* How could you possibly be so irresponsible?"

Holly retreats a few steps, brushing the tears off her cheeks. She looks at the ground. At the wall. At the ceiling. Anywhere but at me.

Jace steps in front of her, holding broad shoulders straight and his chest puffed out. He scowls at me, his eyes burning.

"Leave her alone," he says.

I lift a hand to calm him. "Jace, please stay out of this."

"You shouldn't be yelling at her," Jace says. "It's not her fault."

I gawk at my son, baffled that he could take her side like this, alarmed by how quickly he's willing to turn on his own mother.

"She left the house with my baby and wouldn't answer my calls. That's inexcusable," I say. "Jace, I think you should go to your room. This is a conversation for adults."

"Are you going to fire me?" Holly asks. She appears petite behind my tall twelve-year-old son. She seems younger than her years.

"No, she's not going to fire you." Jace lifts a defiant chin to lock eyes with me. I've never seen him so furious before. With a jolt, I realize his expression reminds me of my dad. Of *me,* even.

I try to calm down. "Before I make any decisions, I need an explanation. And it had better be a good one."

"Why do you have to freak out so much?" Jace yells. "You're so dramatic. It's so embarrassing."

"I'm dramatic because I want to know that my children are safe in the care of a nanny?" I say.

"We are safe," Jace shouts, his face red with anger. "We're here, aren't we?"

Before I can say anything else, Jace storms past me, marching up the steps two at a time.

"Jace, wait," I call after him.

I abandon a sniffling Holly, who is now backed in a corner in the foyer, her arms hooked around her chest.

I jog up the stairs, hurrying to catch up to Jace.

"Just leave me alone!" he screams.

When I reach the landing of the stairs, he rounds the corner and leaps into his room. He slams the door behind him with such force that the pictures on the wall shake.

Lissa is crying so hard she can barely take a breath. Her cheeks are stained with tears. I stroke the dampness away and brush my fingers through her tender blond curls.

"It's all right, baby girl," I whisper into the hollow eave of her ear. "Mommy's here, baby. Jace, please. Talk to me."

"I don't want to talk to you." His voice is muffled through the door. It sounds like he's talking with his face pressed against a pillow.

"I'm sorry." I soften my voice. "Jace, I was scared. Both of my children were missing, and the person I trusted to take care of you wouldn't answer her phone. You understand that, buddy. Don't you?"

"Just go away," Jace says.

"You've never forgotten to come to the shop before, Jace. You used to enjoy it, remember? Come on, please. Don't be mad."

The Nanny's Secret

"I said *go away!*" he shouts.

Defeated, I pad downstairs. The adrenaline lifts off me like steam on a lake. Lissa begins to calm, and I readjust her weight on my hip. Holly is in the kitchen, fixing herself a glass of water. She's no longer crying, but her eyelashes are wet, and her eyes are red rimmed.

"Holly, I'm sorry."

Shyly, she glances up at me. "Don't worry about it. I was in the wrong."

"I… may have overreacted. It looks like I inherited my dad's bad temper after all."

Holly brings the glass to her lips with shaking hands. She takes a short swallow then places the glass down on the counter. "My cell phone died. We came back home to get it once I realized. I think Jace left his phone here, on his nightstand. At least that's what he told me. So that might be why he didn't answer either."

"Why didn't you bring him to the floral shop?"

"We were on our way, but then once I realized my phone was dead and I didn't have the charger, we had to go back."

"Were you already late?" I ask.

"Yeah," she says. "Um, I had trouble soothing Lissa, and then there was traffic. I'm so sorry."

Something about the story doesn't make sense, but I let it go this time because the look in Holly's eyes is genuinely remorseful. Her chin quivers as she says, "I disappointed you, and that's on me. I promise to be more responsible in the future, if you'll give me another chance."

I take a deep breath. "Holly, it's all right."

Her eyes widen, scrolling over me. "Really?"

"You are forgiven."

"Truly?"

"Yes. I know things like this happen. I'm willing to give you another chance. I see you with Lissa and Jace, and I know how much they like you. I don't want to take that away from them."

I nudge my head up toward the stairs and try to smile, although it's painful and probably looks more like a grimace. "He'd probably run away if I let you go now."

Holly tries to smile, too, but the glow doesn't reach her eyes. They're still glossy with tears.

"Thank you. Again, I'm so sorry. I won't let it happen again."

"Let's just forget about it, all right? Or at least try to move on. I'm sorry that I was so aggressive when you walked in the door. I should have let you explain before I went on that rant."

Holly nods, sniffling. "You don't have anything to apologize for. I was in the wrong, but I would like to move past this too."

"I'm going to take Lissa upstairs," I tell her, drained from the fight, feeling like a balloon that's lost all its helium. "Why don't you take a break?"

Holly says, "I can get dinner started if you like."

"Just order a pizza," I tell her. "We all deserve a treat tonight."

Back upstairs, I close my bedroom door and sit on the bed with Lissa still in my arms. I stare up at the ceiling fan,

The Nanny's Secret

the blades whirling, putting me in a trance. What's wrong with me? Why did I blow up at Holly without first getting an explanation? I'm a mess. A tangled bundle of anxiety. Whoever made that picture go viral has already won.

Chapter 10
HOLLY

I wait until I hear Audrey's door close. Then I step softly onto the stairs, taking my time, already familiar with the creaks in the wood, avoiding them.

When I stop outside Jace's room, I listen carefully for any movement from Audrey and Rick's bedroom. The hall is quiet. I can't even hear Lissa babbling. Maybe they fell asleep. If I'm going to make my move, it needs to be now.

Gently, I rap my knuckles against Jace's door.

"Go away," he calls.

I wince, stiffen, and flick my eyes to Audrey's bedroom. The door remains shut.

I lean in and whisper against the wood frame. "Jace? It's me, Holly."

"Holly?" His preteen voice cracks slightly. I hear movement shuffling across the floor. A moment later, the door clicks and opens. Jace stands there blinking. His eyes are red rimmed from tears, but he's not currently crying.

"Can I come in?"

The Nanny's Secret

Jace's eyes narrow. "Where's my mom?"

"In her room, with your little sister." I nudge my chin in the direction of the master suite.

Jace gives me an apprehensive look, as if he's afraid it's a trap and he's going to get in trouble.

"I just want to talk to you." I give him my brightest smile. "It'll only take a second. I promise you're not in any trouble. At least not with me."

He nods and steps aside, letting me into his room.

I close it behind me, quiet as a mouse.

"My mom is going to go batshit if she finds you in here with the door closed," Jace says.

I ignore the swear word and the threat and turn to him, immediately cutting to the chase.

"I know why you're angry," I say.

Jace crosses his arms over his chest. He's a little boy trying to be a man. He tightens his jaw and plants his feet shoulder-width apart. His nostrils flare, and his chin quivers, but he holds firm.

Then it all breaks, and he stares down at his feet. "You couldn't possibly know why."

I step closer to him, guide a hand to his forearm, lightly touch it. I give him a tender look. "Jace, I hated my parents too."

Jace finally meets my eyes. "You did?"

I nod. "They lied to me. They kept secrets from me. I don't know whether it was because they didn't think I would be able to handle the truth, or maybe they were just cowards."

I shake my head and catch myself before I can go too

deep inside my mind again. Jace's brow furrows with concern.

"What happened?" he asks.

I wave a dismissive hand and shift my weight from foot to foot. "That's not important right now." I focus on him, lock eyes with him. The next thing I'm going to say is very important, and I need Jace to understand that I'm an ally, someone he can trust. Someone he can confide in. "Jace, secrets can hurt people. You know that, right?"

Jace's eyes are glassy, staring right through me. I feel sorry for him because he's just a child and the grown-ups around him have let him down. I was like him once. I know exactly how it feels.

"You've seemed kinda mad at your mom recently," I say. "Just like I was mad at my mom when I was your age. That was because my mom kept secrets from me. Is your mom keeping a secret from you too? Is she lying to you?"

A single tear slides down Jace's cheek. He brushes it away and sniffles as he nods again and whispers a single word. "Yes."

I glance back toward the door. The hall is still silent. But I lower my voice just in case.

"This is where I need your help the most," I whisper. "If you tell me your mom's secret, I might be able to fix it."

"I don't know if I should," he says, shaking his head.

"I want to help you," I say. "But I can only do that if you talk to me."

Jace stares at me, his eyes glazing over. He takes a deep breath, and I wait. I've come this far. There's no turning back now.

Chapter 11

Elijah Johnson's hair is the color of a bale of straw if the afternoon sun hits it just right. His blue eyes are sharp and always observing his surroundings, taking everything in, absorbing it all. Elijah Johnson never misses a thing, never skips a beat.

His eyes are so piercing they brighten the space around him. He's forty-five, but his high cheekbones and strong jawline bring out a sense of eternal youth in him. There is not a single wrinkle on his face, not a single hair out of place on his head.

Rick and I always got along with Elijah because he has such a selling force that it's hard to say no to him. Especially when he has a cookout and invites us over and we live next door.

The scent of charcoal and cooked meat floats along the breeze. Elijah blasts reggae music from an outdoor speaker and swings his hips next to the grill. He winks at me and expertly flips a burger. The smile I give him in return is weak.

One smile from Elijah makes a person feel important. Makes them feel like the only person in the room. That's just the way he is. His charm draws people in. It doesn't last forever, though. I know that more than most.

My stomach lurches, and I turn away.

"Can you believe I got that much of a raise?" Elijah laughs. "I mean, I cleaned them out. Took them for what they're worth. That's what you've gotta do with these companies. Show them what you're worth and then take every penny of it because, in the end, you know you're worth it." Elijah's eyes are on Rick, probing, almost daring him to disagree or show any outward sign of contempt.

Rick's trying to be polite and nod along, but his smile looks painful and gritty. His fingers grip the neck of his beer until his thumbnail turns white. He lifts it to his lips and takes a giant swig, swishing it around in his mouth before his throat bobs and he swallows it down.

"Congrats, man. You deserve it," Rick says, hiding his annoyance well.

Elijah, pleased, gives Rick a fond, brotherly slap on the back. "You're damn right I deserve it." He motions with the spatula toward his spacious lawn, which is much bigger than our own. It's also vibrantly green with plush grass that tickles your ankles when you stand in it. "I'm thinking about putting in a pool. Right there. What do you think?"

Rick glances over Elijah's shoulder. I notice my husband bristle, but he concludes with an agreeable and safe response of "That seems like a good spot to put a pool."

The Nanny's Secret

"It'll look pretty good next to my brand-new Range Rover too." Elijah belts out another laugh and jabs Rick in the ribs with his elbow. "I'm just playing around with you, man. I'm very grateful for this life. It's amazing, right? Good food, good company. And if we install a pool back here, you know you and your family are always welcome to use it anytime. Mi casa, su casa. You know how it goes."

That's what Elijah does. He'll say something that will make you want to slap him, but he'll always repair it immediately by saying something that makes him seem generous.

"I was sorry to see that photoshopped picture of you, Audrey," he says, shaking his head. "What's wrong with people?"

"Thanks," I mumble, hoping he'll quickly change the subject. Next to me, Rick bristles. The photograph and the effect it's had on my business is still a sore spot.

Elijah points a spatula at me. "I want you to know that I didn't believe it. Not even for a second. These people are fucking weirdos and not worth your time."

"Thanks so much, Elijah. That means a lot." I take a sip of my wine, spilling a few drops on my dress. I quickly brush them away before anyone notices. "I noticed Emma is getting bigger. Her baby bump, I mean."

Elijah beams. "Another bundle of joy on the way. I can't wait."

Every time his piercing eyes meet mine, I want to look away. It's like looking at the sun too long.

"I think I'll go see if Emma needs any help in the kitchen," I say, longing to get away. "With her growing bump, she must be struggling."

Despite a sigh and a glare from Rick that says, "Don't you dare leave me out here alone with him," I start backing away, toward the house. I mouth a quick "sorry" when Elijah is concentrating on the grill. As I turn my back on them, I see Jace standing awkwardly in the corner of the garden. He's so lanky these days, with his long arms and torso, it's like a punch to the gut. My baby is growing up. But right now, he's frowning at the ground with his hands shoved deep into the front pockets of his jeans. Still a kid who needs me.

"Jace?"

I've been walking on eggshells around him after the incident with Holly the other day. Things are strained, but I'm trying to move past it, and trying my best to show him that I want to be an attentive mom despite my full-time job.

"Hmm?" He blinks up at me, his dark-brown eyes big, brimming with moisture.

"Everything okay?"

Jace lifts one hand to brush his dark hair off his forehead. He shifts his weight, and my heart pangs when I notice his shoulders stiffen.

"Yeah, why?" he asks.

"I just wondered why you aren't upstairs with Asher and Andrew."

Emma and Elijah have four children—two girls and two boys—and another on the way. They haven't found out what gender the new baby will be yet. Emma tells me they want it to be a surprise. She calls this new baby the "tiebreaker" since they already have two of each.

All four of their children have names that start with A,

The Nanny's Secret

which Rick and I find hilarious and have laughed about in private.

"Amber is upstairs with a friend from down the street." Jace shrugs.

Amber is the same age as Jace. They go to school together, and they've always been close. That is, until recently. In fact, Jace hasn't mentioned Amber since Holly arrived. It seems like all the negativity sprouting in my life coincidentally lines up with when I hired her. But as Rick would say, it doesn't mean anything without proof.

"Don't you want to hang out with them?" I ask Jace.

Jace groans. "Fine, if that's what you want."

"Well, no, I just thought—"

Before I can say anything else, Jace spins on a heel and stomps into the house, sliding the patio door too hard. The curtains behind it sway from the force.

I roll my eyes at his back and remind myself to pick my battles. Having a row with Jace in our neighbors' backyard is not something I want to do right now. So, instead, I trot into the kitchen and greet Emma.

"Need any help?" I ask.

Emma lifts her head when she notices me, her cheeks rosy and her forehead a little sweaty. She's placing hot dogs onto a platter to take to the grill.

"Thank you," she breaths out with relief. "Elijah asked me to do all this stuff, and I'm still trying to finish the banana pudding." She points to a casserole dish beside her. "It's coming together, but..." She trails off with an exhausted chuckle.

"What can I do? Can I help you clear up?" I ask.

She places a hand briefly on my arm. "Oh, that would be amazing. Thank you, Audrey."

I start gathering up empty food wrappers and banana peels for the trash.

"Thank you for hosting," I say. "I don't know how you do it all when you're so far along. I'm not pregnant, and I don't have the energy."

"Oh, I don't know," she says. "I guess I just make a lot of very long lists."

Her smile is as humble as a martyr's. Emma is the type of woman who keeps all her worries and frazzled feelings dormant on the inside, making sure they don't show. But I see the fatigue behind her eyes, in her posture. She's a maid, a chauffeur, a baby maker, and a chef. All for her family.

"He enjoys himself anyway," Emma says, glancing at Elijah in the garden, a few people around him. He loves taking center stage, while Emma fades into the background. Still, she seems happy.

My eyes drift to Holly, standing next to Rick. She's laughing at something Rick is saying, and I can tell that she's genuinely amused by him. She tilts her head back and rubs the baby sling, where she's holding Lissa in a wrap. On the surface, her body language is innocuous, but I still watch closely.

Rick leans in, his attention undivided. He has that way about him, that he can make a person feel like they are the only one in the room. His hand cups her shoulder for a moment. My spine straightens. It's nothing. Just a touch.

The Nanny's Secret

And yet it feels like everything. It's such a familiar gesture. One of intimacy. Then Elijah wanders over, and Rick moves away. Holly blushes in response to something Elijah says.

I instinctively glance over at Emma. She's busy with the hot dog placement on the tray. She's not paying attention to her husband outside. I don't know if that's deliberate or if she's really that aloof, but I can't help but sense that Elijah's grin is a bit too frisky and that he may be flirting with Holly. More importantly, is she flirting back? It's too hard to tell. Her expression, although friendly, is still a bit reserved.

"I'm going to bring these out to Elijah." Emma lifts the tray.

"Wait, I can do that for you," I tell her.

Her eyes widen in surprise. I don't know why I feel the sudden urge to protect her. I clasp my hands around the tray and gently coax it from her grasp.

"Really, I don't mind. You should rest. I can come back in and finish the pudding too. Why don't you just sit down on the couch and relax a few minutes?" I look directly at her swollen belly to emphasize what I mean. Emma takes the hint, and her hands steer to her stomach as she absentmindedly strokes the bump.

I glance over my shoulder. Elijah is placing the finished burgers on a clean tray while Holly holds it for him. Their faces and laughter now seem harmless.

"It looks like the burgers might be ready," I say. "I'll get these out there so they can get scorched under the flame real quick. Why don't you just sit under the ceiling fan and embrace the air conditioning until it's all ready? Then I can fix you a plate."

Emma's eyes crinkle at the sides. "Audrey, you really don't have to do all that."

"But I want to." I get the impression that Emma isn't the type of woman who gets pampered often, if at all.

"Oh, sure." She swats her hand through the air. "I'll put my feet up, if only for a few minutes."

"Good for you." I stride to the back door with the tray.

Elijah and Holly glance up when I come out, and Elijah instinctively separates from Holly to a safe arm's length apart. It's such a small, innocuous gesture, and yet I can't help thinking I interrupted something that isn't innocent.

Chapter 12

Elijah thanks me for bringing out the platter, but I can't bring myself to look at him. Instead, my gaze roams over to Holly. She gives me a small smile. As prim as always. And then I walk away.

Elijah is much older than her and married. I don't know what I saw. I also don't know what I saw between Rick and Holly. Now I'm getting paranoid. I'm seeing salacious behavior at every turn when it's really just a touch and some eye contact.

Get a grip, Audrey.

Back in the kitchen, Emma has not taken my advice to sit down and rest. She's back at the counter, slaving over the pudding.

"Hey, I thought we agreed I'm doing that." I gently pry the spoon from her hand. "So, how are you feeling this time around?"

Emma glances down at her stomach as if she's waiting for the correct answer to come to her while staring at it.

"I've had some bloating and some morning sickness issues that have made me a bit uncomfortable." When she lifts her eyes and smiles, I can tell she's trying to mask how bad she really feels.

"Morning sickness is the worst. I was rough for the first sixteen weeks. I got so nauseated whenever I got into a warm shower that I ended up having to take cold showers." I shiver at the memory.

"Odd, isn't it? I'm so glad I'm not the only one."

"No, you're definitely not the only one." I smile. "I hope things improve for you. And I hope Elijah is looking after you. It must be so hard with four kids to look after too."

"Thanks." Emma slices through a banana. "He's doing his best. He works a lot, you know."

I nod. "Rick too. I guess that's what it's like in sales."

Emma smiles. "But we wouldn't have it any other way, would we?"

I return her sweet smile with my own, but under the surface, I find her words are no comfort. And then a sense of sadness washes over me that I haven't felt in a while. The baby I lost. Lissa's sudden arrival afterward. It's fleeting, but it hits me hard.

Elijah makes us both jump when he taps his spatula against the window. "Food's ready out here! Round up the kiddos!"

Even the sound of his voice irritates me.

* * *

The Nanny's Secret

I plonk myself down next to Rick and Jace at the patio table. Holly, on the other side, gives me a little wave. Lissa is already in a high chair, waiting for her food. As everyone digs into the food, I break up little crumbled bits of burger and slice up some strawberries for her.

Rick pours me a merlot, and it goes down smoothly. But I'm still on edge, and I find myself watching Holly, Elijah, and Rick, searching for answers to the questions in my mind. Despite trying to stop my thoughts from going to dark places, I'm convinced that Holly has some ulterior motive for working for us. Whether it's to mess with me or find an older man, I don't know. But I do wonder if I might pick up on vibes as we eat.

Holly's smile is wide and bright as she looks at me. "Would Lissa like some macaroni? Something soft for her to chew on while we eat?"

"Sure. Thanks, Holly." I return the smile, making sure that my thoughts are hidden.

"So, how are you settling into the neighborhood, Holly?" Elijah asks. "I hope we're a friendly bunch."

I notice Holly avoids Elijah's eye contact. "Oh, it's lovely, thank you. Audrey and Rick have been so welcoming."

"And me," Jace says.

Holly smiles. "And you, Jace."

I sip my wine. It rankles that Holly is the only person Jace likes right now.

"Where are you from, Holly?" Elijah asks.

"Not far away," Holly says, readjusting her weight in the seat. "I'm local."

It's interesting to me that Holly is answering in the vaguest of terms. And that she seems so uncomfortable with the questions.

"Didn't go to college, huh?" Elijah says, chewing on his burger. "You seem like a bright young thing, though."

"I'm saving up," she says. "I'm going to do a few years of nannying and then apply."

"That's smart." Elijah points at Holly then vaguely addresses the table. "Don't you think that's smart? Get ahead of the debts."

Frustratingly, Elijah has moved the conversation back to himself and his wisdom. But I glance over at Holly to see how she reacts to Elijah's advice. She's nodding along, seemingly listening to Elijah speak. And then my gaze travels down to Holly's hands. She often places her hands in her lap when she sits. But today her hands are wrapped around the edge of the table. And she's gripping the table so hard that her knuckles are white.

I'm still watching Holly's body language when Lissa spits up some food before starting to cry.

"I can go clean her up if you like?" Holly suggests.

I shake my head. I would rather it be me if one of us leaves. I need some quality time with my baby. "That's okay. You finish your food."

I lift Lissa onto my hip and grab the diaper bag. Rick's eyes seem misty as he watches me leave. Maybe it's been a while since he saw me tend to our baby.

As soon as I'm inside the house alone, some of the tension leaves my body. I hadn't realized just how stiffly I was holding myself throughout the cookout. I set Lissa down on a blanket on the floor in the living room and give her a handful of toys to choose from. She takes a crinkly elephant toy and bashes it around in her dimpled fist, but fat tears still pool in her eyes, and her pink mouth twists into a frown. She keeps crying, uninterested in the toys. I pick her up and walk around in the living room with her, bouncing with her and trying to soothe her.

It doesn't help, so I sit next to her and point to shapes and colors, reciting them all, wondering how much of it she's retaining. Her gray eyes sparkle as though storm clouds are swirling around inside them.

In the short amount of time Holly has lived with us, I notice that it's now getting harder for me to soothe Lissa, and that whenever Holly picks her up if she's fussy or crying, Lissa calms down almost immediately.

I lift Lissa again and let her gnaw on my finger until her crying fades into sighs. A sense of calm washes over me.

"We're just fine on our own, aren't we, monkey?" I murmur.

Her eyelids start to flutter and close, and I cocoon her into the baby wrap and beam when she snuggles close to me. She burrows her tiny body deeper into the wrap, her warm head close to my chest. I want her to remember and be familiar with my scent, too, not just Holly's.

With a little more wind in my sails, I return outside with a sleeping Lissa swaddled to my front. I step outside and slide the door closed. Emma bends over the patio table with a cloth. The kids are playing in the yard. Elijah sings out of tune as he scrubs the grease residue off the grill.

The sky is fading from a pastel pink to a silver gray as

dusk settles in over the neighborhood. It's a perfect night. At least it should be perfect. It's me stopping it being that way by feeling so off-kilter.

Then I look to my right and notice Rick and Holly. They are standing off to the side, in the back corner of the yard. Rick has a goofy grin on his face, and Holly is laughing. Rick isn't leering or touching her. Nor is he leaning in, invading her personal space like Elijah had done back at the grill.

And yet...

Why is he making her laugh so much? Why is she making him smile?

The kids are kicking a soccer ball around them, but jealousy penetrates my body. I worry that it's only a matter of time before the jagged cracks in my foundation start to crumble and collapse around me.

And how am I going to stop it from happening?

Chapter 13

I pull in a shivering breath and lay Lissa down on the changing table, talking to her in a melodic, soothing voice. She gurgles a little then grabs the portable wipes to make the packaging crinkle. This is what matters. My rainbow baby. Nothing could replace the baby I lost before Lissa, but having her here is a joy. Sometimes I wonder if the beautiful boy I lost sent Lissa to me himself as a gift.

Rick has never cheated. Why am I jealous?

It's stress. Nothing more, nothing less. Being here—in this house, with Emma's pregnancy so visible—is doing strange things to my head. It's making me crazy. And who could blame me for feeling a little crazy considering the week I've had?

As I take away the dirty diaper, I notice her bottom is red and swollen. When I try to touch it with the baby wipe, Lissa cries and arches her back, lifting her hips off the changing pad.

I wince, sucking in a deep breath. A thread of pain goes through me just looking at it. I do my best to pat her dry and clean her up without making her suffer too much. I use a generous slather of rash cream that seems to help, but Lissa still doesn't like it when I touch the tender area.

Why is her skin so sore? Annoyed, I strap on a new diaper, working too quickly, fumbling with the edges. My heart beats faster. Anger builds up from the pit of my stomach. Holly hasn't mentioned any kind of rash to me. There's no reason why my baby should be in pain. By the time the diaper is on, my cheeks are as hot as flames.

"Come on, sweetheart." Gently, I collect Lissa into my arms and make my way downstairs.

I can practically feel steam coming out of my pores when I march across the lawn and find Holly still laughing with my husband. How dare she?

"Holly," I bark. "I need to speak to you right now."

Her eyes narrow slightly, confused. "Of course, Audrey, I—"

"How could you not notice?" I snap.

"Notice what?" Holly's jaw drops.

"Honey, are you okay?" Rick takes a step forward and tries to reach for me, but I move away.

"My baby has a terrible diaper rash," I say. "Why didn't you tell me? She's been fussy all day, and it's because she's in pain. What were you thinking, Holly? It's so... so unprofessional of you to allow this to happen."

Despite recent events, I've never been one for confrontation, and now my heart is hammering against my ribs. I don't like myself as I stare at this young woman,

The Nanny's Secret

my eyes burning into hers. I can tell I'm hurting her feelings, but maybe that's why I'm doing it. Because I need to lash out at someone else before I burst out of my own skin.

Holly's eyes brim with tears. "I— I didn't... I'm so sorry. I didn't—"

Someone clears his throat behind me, and when I turn around, I see Elijah hovering. "Is there a problem, Audrey?" He lets out an awkward burst of laughter. "Because you're kind of killing the mood here."

"It's a personal issue," I say, glaring at him.

For once Elijah reads the room and backs away. Still, I can't stop staring at him, following the shape of his back as he walks toward Emma. Her regards me too. As do my husband and son. Everyone is looking at me like I'm the freak show.

I aim a scathing glare at Holly. "I pay you to take care of my baby, not hurt her."

"Audrey!" Rick steps forward and takes my arm. "I think we should leave. Now. Come on. It can't be as bad as all that."

"She has a rash, Rick—"

"Yeah, babies get rashes," he says. "Jace had rashes when he was a baby too. Did that mean you weren't looking after him?"

"This rash has been there for a few days." I yank my arm from his grip. "And Holly hasn't bothered to tell me."

"It's my fault, Rick." Holly turns to me. "I'm so sorry. I didn't realize the rash had gotten worse. I put cream on it this morning, but I must have forgotten to check again—"

"Probably because you were too busy joking around with my husband," I say.

Holly stares at me as though I've slapped her in the face. "That's not... I wasn't."

"For God's sake, Audrey." Rick places his hands on his hips and glances over at Elijah and Emma, who are now pointedly not looking at us.

Jace steps over and stands near Holly. His face is pale, and I think for a moment he's going to defend her again. But he seems to think better of it when he sees the furious expression on my face.

"I'm sorry," Holly says, quickly brushing away a tear. "I should go."

Before anyone can say anything else, she hurries across the lawn away from us. All at once, the breath in my lungs suddenly releases. I worry that my bones might melt, and I'll wilt into a puddle of goop and mush, seeping into the grass.

As soon as Holly is gone, Rick leans in so close that I can smell the beer and the burger on his breath.

"Audrey," he hisses again. "What the hell has gotten into you? You made a scene in front of our neighbors, all because of a diaper rash? What the actual fuck?"

"I... I don't know, Rick." I touch my fingers to the top of my forehead. My skin is clammy and hot and feels like it doesn't belong to me. It's too loose, but it's also too tight. "I lost my head."

"You think?" He raises his eyebrows. There is stillness in his anger. Like he's the freezing cold to my volcano.

"I went upstairs to change Lissa's diaper, and the rash

looked so bad, Rick. So bad. And Holly never said a word to me. Doesn't that piss you off?" I match his stare.

He sighs. "I get it. I really do. But we both know it wasn't serious enough to warrant all this." He gestures vaguely around him. "Screaming at a young nanny. Embarrassing us in front of our friends. Look, I know things have been hard recently, but you really need to get your temper in check."

I nod. "I know."

He places his hands on his hips. "What's bringing all this on? You've been snapping a lot lately. You need to talk to me."

"What? And have you tell me I'm running my floral shop into the ground?" I snap.

His voice is clipped when he replies. "That's not what I said."

"I'm just stressed, Rick. Someone is out to get me. I might even lose my shop because of that stupid viral photo. And..." My chin wobbles when tears threaten to spill over. "Ever since Holly arrived, I feel like I'm being replaced. Even Lissa soothes more easily with Holly around."

"Well, Holly isn't perfect," Rick says. "That's pretty obvious from what has happened today. You're right. She should have told us both about the rash, especially if it's as bad as you said. And she shouldn't have left the house without a phone charger the other day. She's made some mistakes, and maybe we need to make it clear that isn't acceptable. Unless you want to find someone else."

"I mean, she'll probably leave after today," I say. "I know I would."

Finally, Rick places an arm over my shoulder. Lissa nuzzles against my chest, and I lean into my husband. The heat and anger seep out of me, and I'm left with an unnerving numbness. Jace stares at me, a wary expression on his face. I've let him down again. I've let them all down.

Rick strokes my back. "No one could ever replace you. I hope you know that."

"I saw you two laughing and talking alone. I thought you were flirting," I admit. "It really messed with my head."

He laughs. "Oh, come on, darling. Why would I be interested in her? I've got a piece of prime rib at home." He winks.

Despite it all, it coaxes a laugh out of me. He hugs me close and kisses the top of my head, and a tingle spreads through my body.

I turn around and give Emma and Elijah a little wave.

"Sorry about that," I say. "Just some nanny business."

Emma steps forward, rubbing her pregnant belly. "Is everything okay?"

"Just a miscommunication," I say. "Lissa has a bad diaper rash I didn't know about. It caught me off guard. I'm so sorry about ruining your cookout."

Elijah moves closer, too, and strokes Lissa's forehead. "Poor baby."

I want to pull Lissa away from him, but I quell the urge.

"Oh, that would bother me too," Emma says. "Goodness, Audrey, I don't know how you allow a stranger to look after your children. I wouldn't be able to cope with it."

My smile thins. "Well, I'm obviously not coping with it well." I wipe the dampness from my eyes with the heel of my palm. "I think we're going to head home. I'm so sorry for the outburst. Thank you for an otherwise lovely barbeque."

Rick motions to Jace, and I watch my son drag his feet over to us. The look in Jace's eyes makes my blood run cold. No one hates you more than an adolescent. I just hope there's love in there too.

Elijah, on the other hand, looks at me as if I've grown two heads. His eyes follow me as I walk toward the house—narrowed, curious, concerned. I feel his stare burning into me all the way to the back door. Even though I try to ignore it, and even though Rick's comforting hand is resting on my lower back as he guides me inside, I can't.

"Maybe they won't invite us next time," Rick says as we make our way back up our drive. "So, you know, you might have actually done us a favor."

I elbow him gently in his side. I would even enjoy this moment if it weren't for Jace's icy expression. Then there's the awkward conversation with Holly that awaits me once we get home. Part of me hopes she might quit today and save us both a load of trouble later. If I fire her now, Rick will think I've become irrational, and Jace will hate me even more than he does already. And if Holly is a malevolent presence in my household, what will she do to us if we fire her? What kind of revenge will she bring down on my family?

Chapter 14
HOLLY

It takes a while to burn off the residual rage, but walking quickly around the park helps. I keep going over the barbecue in my mind, every moment. Every laugh, every touch, and then Audrey's outburst at the end. The problem is, Audrey can sense that I'm here for a reason other than looking after her children. And, yeah, maybe I took my eye off the ball. But taking care of a baby is new to me. I was hoping the rash would clear up before she noticed.

Now she might fire me. And I haven't finished what I started.

The sky above is gray, the color of ash and soot. It's cloudless, but I feel like the air is thick with the threat of an incoming storm. I find a vacant bench and sit to get my heart rate back to a regular rhythm. There's the distant hum of traffic, the birds chirping, the sound of running shoes on pavement.

I pull my phone out of my purse and swipe to the text

The Nanny's Secret

app. I take a deep breath, staring at the screen for a few moments, and then I start typing out a message.

I think Audrey is going to be a problem. She keeps watching me like a hawk, so I need to be careful. But he was definitely flirting with me.

I take another deep breath, willing the three little dots to pop up in their little gray bubble on the screen.

It's both an eternity and an instant when it happens.

Promise me you'll keep yourself safe. I think what you have planned is really dangerous.

I type out an immediate response and send it this time, with no hesitation.

Don't worry. I have it under control. Jace is the key in all this. What he told me the other day changes everything.

A few moments later comes another reply.

Don't underestimate him.

Chapter 15

After a decent night's sleep, I decide that Holly deserves a second chance. Rick thinks the same, though I do believe he also thinks I'm a bit crazy at the moment. And maybe he's right. I've been through a lot of stress. My instincts aren't to be trusted while I have all this adrenaline coursing through my veins. I'm in survivor mode, fresh from the awful viral photo and the damage to my business. Not to mention how weird it is to have a stranger in my house, looking after my kids.

Emma was sort of right with that one. She meant it as a dig. But she wasn't wrong. I'm not handling the transition well.

To help smooth things over, I have coffee with Holly the next morning and do my best to sincerely apologize. With Rick in the office again this Sunday, we have plenty of time for a chat. We convene in the kitchen, and I make us both matcha lattes as a treat.

"I really appreciate you giving me a second chance,"

The Nanny's Secret

Holly says. She's in a polka dot dress today with her hair pulled away from her face by an Alice band. She seems younger than ever. The paranoid part of my brain wonders if she styled herself this way on purpose, to make herself seem like less of a threat.

"We do like you, Holly. We're just a bit worried about your communication. I want to be in the loop for everything. Okay?"

"Okay," she says.

"Oh. I also went to the store yesterday and grabbed some stronger rash cream." I grab the pot from my purse. "Try this. It worked wonders on Jace when he was a baby."

"Thank you," she says. "And again, I'm really sorry. It was all my fault. You're right, I should have told you, and I swear I'm going to work on communication." She lets out a long sigh of relief. "I thought you brought me to the kitchen to fire me, to be honest. I'm so glad I was wrong. I need this job. And I love the kids so much."

"Well, I handled things badly. I flew off the handle, and I shouldn't have." I sip my latte. "So maybe we're even."

"I'll go and try out this cream right now—"

I place out a hand to stop her. "No, finish your latte first. Lissa's napping anyway."

She sips the drink. "This is delicious, by the way."

I smile. "Thanks, that's so sweet." And then I decide to use this moment to learn more about Holly. I caught a few glimpses at the barbeque, but I sense there are more layers. Now would be a good time to learn as much from her as I can. "So, where are you thinking of going to college? Have you applied anywhere yet?"

She shakes her head. "I'm still considering my options. But I don't want to move too far away."

"And you're a local? You grew up around here?"

She nods.

"So you went to Georgetown High?"

She nods again. "I saw old Mr. Krasinski when I picked up Jace the other day. Looks like he's still teaching math. He wasn't my favorite, but then I wasn't very good at math." She laughs, and it sounds slightly forced.

I can't help but wonder if she knows I'm testing her. Jace loves Mr. Krasinski and may have pointed him out before. I wish I could find a way to know for sure, but Rick and I moved here from out of town. I decide to push the conversation in a different direction.

"Are you good with computers, Holly?" I place the latte down on a coaster and smile at her.

"Not really," she says. "I can do the basics. Like post on social media or research a paper. Why do you ask?"

I sigh. "Well, I reported the photo, the death threats, and the graffiti to the police last week, and I haven't heard anything back about it. So I was hoping, since you found the original image so quickly, that you might be able to uncover the IP address of the person who uploaded the photo to Twitter."

"Oh, I don't think so." She shakes her head. "All I did was a reverse image search on Google to find the still from the movie. I don't think I can do anything as complex as what you're asking."

"Do you know anyone who might?" I ask.

She shakes her head. "No, sorry. The police should be

doing that for you, though. Maybe you should chase them up."

I sigh. "You might be right." Then I lean forward. "If this had happened to you, what would you do?"

She fingers the rim of the glass before answering. "Well, I'd be feeling pretty paranoid. But I'd probably let the police handle it."

"Yeah, maybe you're right." I finish the rest of the latte and take my glass over to the sink to rinse. "I'm so glad we had this chat, Holly. I wanted to clear the air after everything at Elijah's." I lean my hip against the kitchen counter. "What do you make of them? Elijah and Emma."

Holly's eyes narrow as they meet mine. "What do you mean?"

I sigh. "We've known Elijah and Emma for a long time now. I..." My mouth suddenly goes dry, I swallow and concentrate on what I'm trying to say. "I sometimes worry about Emma. She goes so unappreciated in that house. Sometimes..." I shake my head, trailing off. "Ah, never mind. I'm rambling."

"He definitely seems in control," Holly says. "And he talked a lot about having another boy. It sounds like he really wants one."

"Was he inappropriate with you at all?"

Holly's eyebrows shoot up. "Inappropriate? No, I don't think so. Why?"

"I just wanted to check because he seemed a little over-familiar with you."

She smiles primly. "He was just being friendly. I didn't mind."

"Good." My gaze trails over to the clock on the oven, and I notice that it's almost ten and Jace still isn't out of this bedroom. "Well, I'd best get the preteen up."

"I'll go and apply the rash cream," Holly says, grabbing the tub.

"Not to the preteen, I hope," I say with a laugh. But Holly just looks horrified. I pat her arm to reassure her that I was joking, and then I make my way over to the stairs.

"Jace?" I shout. And then again. I listen carefully. The faint sound of music is coming from his room. "Jace, get down here. I know you're awake."

"What do you want?" he yells back.

"Excuse me?" The aggressive tone hits me like a slap. "You can't talk to me like that. I'm your mother. I said *get down here.*"

I hear his stomps before I see him. Jace stands on the top stair. His clothes are rumpled, his hair a mess. He rubs his red eyes.

"What do you want?" He shrugs as if this is a trivial conversation and he can't wait to get it over with to get back to whatever it was he was doing.

"What I *want* is for you to apologize for talking to me so disrespectfully. Then you can make a start on your chores."

He sighs and clomps his way down the stairs, barely looking at me as he makes his way into the kitchen. Well, at least he's making a start on his chores. He empties the dishwasher, banging the plates around as he stuffs them back into the cupboards.

"Can you please be a little gentler with those before you break them?" I ask.

The Nanny's Secret

Jace finally meets my gaze. His eyes are sadder than I expect them to be, creasing in the corners.

"I'm doing what you asked me to do, aren't I?" he says.

"That's it, Jace. Last straw. You're grounded. No baseball practice and no going over to friends' houses."

His jaw drops. He wasn't expecting me to play that card.

"Mom, you can't be serious. We have an important game this weekend. I have to be at the practice!"

I almost falter. I know how much it means to him, but if I become a pushover and don't follow through, he'll know he'll be able to stretch the boundaries for the next time.

"I'm sorry, Jace, but you need to be more respectful, and you need to learn not to talk to me that way. I don't know what's going on with you lately, but the attitude you've been giving me is unacceptable, and I cannot condone it any longer."

"What are you even talking about?" Jace shrieks.

"Bad behavior has to be punished."

"I'm not six years old," he snaps.

"Then act like it! Prove to me that you're mature and that you and I can be civilized to each other. Then I'll think about ungrounding you."

"This house is a prison, and I can't stand it," Jace yells. He slams a cupboard so hard I think it might come off the hinges.

"Oh, come on, Jace." I take a step toward him. "I'm not asking for much, am I? I'm your mom, remember?"

But he ignores me and barrels past, almost clipping my shoulder as he rounds the counter to march back upstairs.

"Don't slam your door," I shout as I hear him climbing the stairs.

He slams it anyway. I run a hand through my hair. I don't know what has gotten into him recently, but I don't like it.

Chapter 16

I'm working on a floral arrangement at the store the next morning, and the world is finally beginning to feel normal again. We have new orders. I've settled things with Holly. Jace isn't talking to me, but he's behaving better and is at least clearing up after himself after our fight. And then my phone dings. I snatch it up from the worktable and spot an email notification alert.

Smiling to myself when I see the order details in the subject line, I quickly open it to see what the client would like. And then I notice that the body of the email is written in all caps in bold red type—bright red, murder red, furious red.

You've got some nerve, bitch. Count your blessings. And your days. You'll get what's coming to you.

An icy chill claws its way down my spine. I shudder. As soon as I place my phone down, I pick it back up and read the message again. Then a third and a fourth time. Each time I read it, the ache in my stomach widens, like a gaping pit. I take a deep breath as my pulse starts to race, swooshing across my eardrums.

"Everything okay?"

I jump nearly a foot when I hear Serena's voice behind me. She's standing in the doorway to the workshop, a confused wrinkle zigzagging across her forehead.

"Serena." My voice is breathless. I place a palm against my chest. "I didn't see you come in."

"I brought back a half sandwich for you." She holds up a brown paper bag. "Ham and cheese. And that blueberry muffin you asked for."

My memory jogs. "Right." I attempt to smile. "That's right. Thank you. Sorry, I'm a bit spooked. I just got another of those threatening emails."

"Shit." Serena hands me my change along with the bag. "Have you heard anything from the police?"

"No, nothing." I pull the sandwich out of the bag. "I guess I'll forward it on." I give her a bright smile that I don't feel. "They're just empty threats, right? None of these clowns have the balls to actually do anything."

Serena nods. "Exactly. They're just bored people."

"I'm fine, really." I point to the arrangement I'd been working on. "Can you finish that up for me now that your lunch break is over? The instructions are on the order sheet next to it on the table. I'm going to go eat this in my office."

Serena nods, some of the wariness in her eyes fading as she pushes her purse into the cubby underneath the register and heads to the workshop.

I take a deep breath and go to my office, sealing the door shut behind me. I need to get myself—and this situa-

The Nanny's Secret

tion in general—under control before someone gets hurt. Maybe before I get hurt.

Just as I thought things were calming down... It's like I'm pushing a rock up a hill, slipping and faltering before getting back up and carrying on. When is it going to stop? I sit down at my desk chair and take three deep breaths then pull up the email on my computer screen. The email is even more intimidating on the larger device. The red is redder. The all-caps letters scream at me.

Serena and I talked about these anonymous emails like they're coming from strangers, but when I read them, they feel personal. I shake the thought out of my head, close the threat, and find the number for the police station on my phone.

A female receptionist answers on the third ring. At first, she sounds overwhelmed and overworked, but once I start explaining my situation to her, her voice changes from frazzled indifference to concerned.

"One moment, Mrs. Miller. I'll transfer you to a detective. If you get a voice mail, leave a message, and someone will call you back within twenty-four hours. We're really swamped right now, but we take every case seriously and do our best to keep the lines of communication open."

"It's just that I reported this a week ago, and it's still going on."

"I understand that," she says. "One moment, and I'll put you through."

I thank her and nod along to the elevator music. Sure enough, I get a generic voice mail of a detective named Todd Stalks. Trying to speak clearly, I go through the whole spiel again of the photo and the threats, explaining that I'd love to track the IP address to figure out who it is. I leave my name and number then hang up. It's all I can do.

Now I have to wait and hope someone will get back to me sooner rather than later. I stare at the computer screen but click out of the email browser. I can't look at it anymore. It's making me sick.

* * *

We order pizzas in the evening, and Holly eats with us. I don't tell Rick about the email. Instead I focus on the new orders coming into the floral shop. Ever since he talked about me possibly selling the shop, I've only wanted to tell him good things. Positive things. I know I should admit to my husband that I'm still receiving threats, but I don't want him to know the store is still in jeopardy.

After dinner, Holly shows me the progress of Lissa's diaper rash, and I'm relieved to see some real improvement. It seems as though Holly is following the instructions well, and the cream is doing its job. Despite the threatening email looming over my thoughts, I go to bed feeling positive.

"You look good tonight," Rick says, pulling me onto his lap as he sits on the edge of the bed. "Is this new?" He runs a finger under the hem of my nightgown.

It's not. He's seen it many times, but I nod anyway. "I bought it because I thought you'd like it."

"I'd like it on the floor even more," he murmurs, nuzzling into my neck.

The Nanny's Secret

Every part of my body runs hot. Some of that adrenaline that's been coursing through me finally has an outlet. My hands work faster than his to pull down his pajama bottoms. He grunts in pleasure as I lower myself down onto him. I grind my hips, then he lifts me, pushes me down on the bed, and thrusts hard into me until we both collapse.

"Oh fuck, Audrey, I've missed you," he says, grabbing my breasts.

Before I drift off to sleep, I think to myself that it has been a while since we made love. Rick works late and is often tired. So was I with Lissa always on my hip, and then since I started back at work, the long hours have tired me out. It's good to know he still wants me and that I can still tingle all over from his touch.

We straighten the bedding, climb in, and go to sleep. And as I drift off, a deep sense of guilt and shame washes over me. A guilt that I thought I'd buried. One from my past that lurks below the surface, always there. Luckily, I'm asleep before it consumes me.

The next morning, I'm on my way to work, trying to navigate the heavy rush hour traffic, sip my tumbler of coffee I brought from home, and turn the wheel.

My phone rings. It's a number I don't recognize. I hit the Bluetooth button. "Hello?"

A man clears his throat. "Is this Audrey Miller?"

"Yes?"

"This is Detective Stalks returning your call about an IP address."

"Oh! Right. Yes. That was me who called." I turn onto

the side street leading to the floral shop. "Did I also speak to you about the photo and the graffiti?"

"No, that was an officer, but I've been catching up on it," he says.

"I've kept every threatening email since then. I received another one yesterday, and it scared me a bit. I wondered if you'd figured out who uploaded the photo. Did you get an IP address or anything?"

I hear rustling on the line, as if Detective Stalks is sorting through a stack of paper documents. "Unfortunately, I ran out of leads on this one."

"You couldn't find the source?"

He clears his throat again. "No, ma'am. I apologize for that. I had my team look into it, and the problem is, whoever the emailer is covered their tracks pretty well."

"Sorry, this is all new to me. Can you explain what that means?"

I park behind the building, trying to trap the panic stirring in my stomach.

"The Twitter account used a VPN to hide the user's identity. This is otherwise known as a virtual private network. It routes your Internet activity through an encrypted connection so that no one else will be able to track what you're doing or be able to track the location of the device you're working from. Now, some of the threats came from traceable accounts, and we will be speaking to those people. But the original account and the email address for the most recent email both used VPNs."

"Oh." My stomach falls down to my feet. "So there's no way of finding them?"

The Nanny's Secret

"Wait just a moment before you hang up." Detective Stalks muffles the phone and coughs away from the receiver. "Save my number, the one I'm calling you from. That's my personal cell. I would like you to keep track of any other threats you receive. You can call me with them, and if we're able to nail anything down, we'll look into it."

"Okay, yeah. For sure. I will absolutely do that. Thanks so much for that. That's very good advice."

"No problem. In the meantime, stay safe, and be alert. Carry pepper spray with you to feel safe when you're alone if you need to. You might want to think about additional security at your store and home."

"Like what?" I ask.

"Security cameras and alarms would be a good start."

"We have an alarm and a camera inside and outside the shop."

"But the outdoor cameras were not good quality. I remember that because we couldn't get a decent image of the person who vandalized your store," he says.

"You think I should replace them?"

"I do," he says.

"I'll get right on it."

"And we will attempt to work around the VPN if we can. I'll let you know if there are any further updates. All right?"

"I appreciate it."

I hang up. It's better than nothing but not what I'd hoped. And at least I have something actionable to do.

Chapter 17

Finally, I have a normal day. No more death threats or graffiti. No incidents with Jace or Holly. Blossoms and Bouquets receives a new wedding order with a request for black roses. Serena and I have had a blast creating designs for the Goth wedding, and we're both dying to see the finished results.

On the way home, I call and let Holly know I'll be late. I have a few errands to run, and I'd like her to make a start on dinner. Then I drive across town to the hardware store. Detective Stalks was right. I do need better security both at work and at home. I make my way down the aisles until I find the security cameras.

One of the assistants helps me with outdoor cameras. I get two for the store and two for home. Then I come across a row of cameras hidden inside stuffed toys.

"Are these those nanny cams I saw advertised?" I ask.

The assistant, a young guy with red hair, picks one up. "That's right, ma'am. They're very discreet. This one has

The Nanny's Secret

an app so that you can view the footage on your phone. It's a great way to keep track of the little ones when you're not in the room. And these..." He reaches up to a higher shelf. "These are shaped like a smoke alarm or a lightbulb so they don't stand out in the home."

"I had no idea." I take the box with the lightbulb camera inside it from the assistant. "It's like a spy setup."

He nods. "That's exactly what they are. Though I do have to warn customers that it's illegal to record someone without their consent." He winks at me conspiratorially, like he thinks I'll be using the camera for nefarious means.

But perhaps he's right. Because I have an idea.

* * *

"Hello?" I call out to an empty, quiet kitchen, tossing my car keys into the wicker basket on the counter and shrugging off my purse strap. "Rick? Holly?"

Silence. Then laughter in the garage behind me.

I spin and face the still-open door, finding Rick and Holly sidling up the driveway. Rick has both hands curled around the handle of the stroller. He's giving Holly a broad smile, his caramel eyes flaring up with as much light as the late-afternoon sun.

Holly's gaze is on him, too, her grin wide, her posture at ease. She's wearing a pink sports tank top and black jogging shorts. A far cry from the modest way she usually dresses.

Her shiny hair is pulled up into a high ponytail that bounces and sways with each step she takes. Her face is flushed pink from exertion.

Holly sees me standing there in the doorway, and for a fleeting sliver of a second, so quick I start to wonder if I imagined it, a darkness brims in her expression. It fades away as fast as it appeared.

I absentmindedly adjust my dress, pressing my palms to the pleats and wrinkles that have occurred from a day at work. I don't know why I have the sudden urge to breeze over to Rick and kiss him like I'm some sort of territorial animal. I glance down at my curvy hips, the doughy softness of my belly, secretly comparing them to Holly's thinner frame and flat-as-a-board, twenty-something stomach.

I lick my lips and straighten my shoulders, allowing my face to compose itself into a welcoming smile, ignoring the shortcomings and loneliness festering inside me.

Rick stops inside the garage, casts me a wave, and declares in a breathless voice, "Hey, Aud."

My heart flutters at the affectionate shortening of my name that he hasn't used in months. "How's it going?"

He steps around the side of the stroller and carefully lifts out a sleeping Lissa. He cradles her against his chest. Her chubby arm dangles down, her pink mouth open slightly from restful slumber.

"Great." My voice is an unused, rusty wheel. I clear my throat and try again. "I just got home from the hardware store. I spoke to a detective today. He thinks I should replace the security cameras outside Blossoms and Bouquets. Oh, and I got a few for outside the house too."

"A detective," Rick says. "For the photograph?"

"And the graffiti and the death threats," I remind him.

The Nanny's Secret

He seems surprised someone is actually looking into it. And then I bristle, wondering if he's even taking this seriously.

"We don't need cameras at the house though, do we?" he asks. "Isn't that overkill?"

I glance across at Holly, who must be taking in this tension between husband and wife.

"I don't think so," I say.

"Okay, well, whatever makes you feel safe," he says.

I don't tell him about the other cameras I bought from the store. Instead, I decide to change the subject. "Where have you guys been?"

"We went for an evening walk," Holly answers before Rick does. A glossy layer of sweat is gleaming across her neck and collarbone, but she wears it well, looking fresh and shimmery.

"Oh?" I study Rick, trying to keep my eyebrows from lifting off my forehead.

"Just around the neighborhood." Holly bites off a piece of granola bar out of her tiny backpack. Her voice is seamless, smooth, casual. "We went to the park. Lissa played on the swings. She giggled every time Rick swung her high."

I look from Holly to Rick, knowing he can see the perplexed expression contorting my face because he frowns. There's even a hint of guilt that flashes across his eyes.

"Since when do you go on neighborhood walks and to the park?" I try to keep my voice light and teasing. It sounds false even to my ears.

Rick never goes on walks with me, even when I suggest

them. In fact, I stopped asking him a long time ago because he always gave me some excuse.

I'm too tired. I just want to watch baseball. I was getting ready to cut the grass. I want to grill out instead. Honey, just let me relax; it's been a long day.

Heaven forbid he take a stroll with me and his infant daughter. But now that the nanny is here, he's all for it? Something isn't quite right about this picture, but maybe, yet again, I'm reading too much into it.

Rick shrugs, stroking his fingers across sleeping Lissa's back. "Holly suggested we go out and get some fresh air and exercise. I figured I might as well join her, seeing as you said you'd be out late. Lissa was kind of fussy. Holly thought maybe the walk around the block would help calm her down. Then we ended up at the park."

"And now she's asleep," Holly declares with a boastful smile as if she's the cure to every problem.

"Maybe she was cranky because of her rash?" I can't help myself. Rick gives me a cautious glance.

"It's clearing up," Holly says. "In fact, it's almost gone now."

"Good."

"Well, anyway," Rick says, "I was thinking about making dinner tonight. Who wants steak?"

"I do!" Holly exclaims. "Need any help? Jace tells me you're a grilling master."

I wince and turn to follow them, once again feeling like the third wheel in my own home.

Rick's chest puffs out at the compliment. He pretends to be humble, swatting an indifferent hand through the air.

"Well, I don't know about all *that*, but I can show you some tricks of the trade if you're interested."

"Absolutely," Holly says, a little too enthusiastically for my liking.

I should like Holly. I should be relieved that she's fitting in so well with my family. Why is it so hard for me to be a better person?

Rick places Lissa in her swing and sets the rocker to the lowest setting. Lissa stirs a bit, but when Rick places a blanket over her lap, she stays asleep. He sets his phone down on the counter and starts digging around in the fridge and pantry for spices and seasonings for the steaks.

"I'm going to grab a quick shower," Holly says.

"Sure." I smile and grab a seat by the breakfast bar, hoping Rick and I can have a little alone time before dinner.

"Actually, hon, I think I might change while the steaks are resting." He plants a kiss on the top of my head and hurries up the stairs, leaving his phone behind.

His *phone*.

I stare at it on the counter. It's there, baiting me. It's like a test from the universe. I have two options. Pass or fail. I'm already spiraling enough. I already have spy cameras in my car that I intend to set up so I can watch the nanny.

Fuck it. I'm already in too deep.

I snatch the phone up.

Then I set it back down and huff out a deep, frustrated breath. I glance at the stairs. I can't hear any talking. Lissa's swing clicks, rocking back and forth, a lulling sound. The steaks are resting on the counter, coming to room temperature. Rick always says they cook more evenly on the grill at room temperature.

If Rick had anything to hide, he wouldn't have inadvertently left his cell phone downstairs where I could search through it at my leisure. He would use any excuse to keep it close at hand, never letting it out of sight. Wouldn't he?

I love my husband. I trust my husband. Maybe I should just relax and pour myself a glass of wine, sit out on the back deck, and watch him grill a delicious dinner for us. I am lucky to have such an involved husband that he takes a walk with Lissa and the nanny to spend time with our daughter.

I step away from the phone and reach for the bottle of red sitting on the counter, pour it into a glass, and take a sip. It warms my insides almost instantly, and I release a soft, relaxed sigh.

So what if Rick and Holly went on a walk together? It's an innocent activity. I tell myself not to be so paranoid and take another sip of the wine, easing myself into the peaceful evening I desperately need. Besides, I'll soon set up the cameras inside the house so that I can know for sure whether Holly is trying to steal my husband.

Chapter 18

Rick stares down at the box with the security camera inside. He picks it up and turns it over. "Are these really necessary?"

I resist the urge to snatch the box from his hand. "I've had death threats, Rick."

He places the box down on the dining table. Lissa, sitting in her high chair, reaches out for it with a chubby hand.

"You're right. Sorry," Rick says. "I've just always hated that paranoia, you know? That everyone is out to get us. It's why I never wanted a gun in the house."

As soon as he says the word, my mind begins to whir. It's true that Rick has always viewed the world with rose-tinted glasses. He would rather see the good in people than the bad. I'm more of a realist. And now I'm wondering if a gun might be a good idea. I didn't grow up in a household with a gun. Mom never let Dad buy one. Possibly because of his temper. Dad had never physically hit anyone, but he could scream and shout at times. Which is also a good argument against me getting a gun, seeing as I have a little of his temper.

I would also need to learn how to use it.

"I wouldn't be doing this if I wasn't worried," I say. "It's just a surveillance camera. If anyone decides to spray-paint Cat Killer or whatever on the house, at least we'll catch them doing it."

"I get it. Anyway, I have to run to work. Are you okay installing this?" He plants a kiss on my forehead.

"Holly's going to help. I'm taking the morning off work and then setting up the cameras at the shop this afternoon."

"Sounds like you've got things under control, babe." He grabs his briefcase. He plants a second kiss on Lissa's forehead. "See you later."

I watch him leave, and for the briefest of moments, I wish I had a husband who stayed to fit the security camera for me. Who took these threats seriously. Who wasn't always distracted by work.

And then I look at my daughter, and I push those thoughts aside.

***

The security cameras turn out to be fairly simple to install. Holly does a lot of the manual work, climbing up a stepladder to install the camera above the front door. I also add a doorbell camera and one for the back yard. Then, after I download an app on my phone, everything is good to go.

The Nanny's Secret

"Why don't you grab us some subs for lunch?" I pull a few notes from my wallet. "I think we deserve them."

"Okay, sure," she says, smiling her sweet smile.

Once Holly has backed her car out of the drive, I hurry upstairs with the lightbulb spy cameras I installed. Working quickly, I unscrew the bulbs in Lissa's room, the upstairs corridor, and the living room. And then I pause. Putting one in our bedroom would be an invasion of my husband's privacy. It will record us having sex. But I desperately want to know if Holly goes in our room. Something at the back of my mind is telling me she does.

In the end, I don't do it. I'll be able to see enough from the hallway camera. I don't need one in our room.

Then I head outside to grab the mail, taking Lissa with me on my hip. I open my mailbox and peer in, finding a huge bundle of letters and ad flyers, grumbling to myself about it. Rick usually brings the mail inside, but he's been slacking on it the last few days.

Lissa is fussing, her dimpled fists balled. I bounce her on my hip while pulling the mail out with my free hand.

"Shush, baby," I murmur. "Just give Mommy a minute to go through this junk. Wait till you're older and you have bills to pay. That'll be something, eh? More pizza menus. Damn."

I turn to head back to the house, almost bumping into Elijah mid spin.

"Elijah." I readjust Lissa's weight after jolting her slightly. "You scared me."

"Sorry about that, Audrey." He smiles, light bouncing from his white teeth. He's impeccably groomed as always, in well-fitting jeans and a white shirt. "I didn't mean to startle you."

I wave a hand, trying to remain casual. "It's fine. Don't worry about it."

Elijah leans over Lissa. "What's wrong, little one? Having a rough time?"

My fingers tighten around my daughter's waist. I want to pull her away from him, but I don't. "She's teething."

Elijah squints under the bright sun. "Where's the rest of your clan?"

"Rick's at work, and Jace is at school," I say, trying to keep my tone light. "I have the morning off."

"Cool," he says. "And your sweet little nanny?"

The way he says that makes my skin grow cold. "She's grabbing lunch for us."

"Who's managing the store for you?" he asks.

It's odd he's asking so many questions.

"Serena," I say.

"Ah." Elijah nods, his expression casual and unbothered. He reaches for Lissa, cupping his hands under her arms. "May I?"

I shift my weight, uneasy. "Um, sure."

He's already scooped her into his arms anyway, regardless of my consent, but he sways her back and forth, holding her close like she's a fragile doll.

She stops whining almost immediately. My throat bobs, and my voice is heavy when I get the words out, trying not to sound too uncomfortable. "You're a natural." In spite of myself, I can't deny what's true.

Elijah's eyes pan from the baby to me. His smile gleams

across the whole yard. "Well, I have quite a few of these myself."

He says it as if children are collectible possessions, not real people. I wince when he puts his hand up to the top of her head and brushes his tan fingers through the fine strands.

"Her hair is really light."

"It'll darken eventually. Jace's was light, too, when he was a baby."

Elijah gives me an assessing look. "Pretty like her mama."

I swallow hard and reach for her. Elijah gives her up willingly. He juts a thumb over his shoulder.

Elijah points across to the front door. "Couldn't help noticing you putting up a camera. Smart move. You might want to be careful."

I place Lissa on my hip and turn to him, my skin prickling with gooseflesh. "What do you mean?"

"We just had a break-in." Elijah blows out a deep breath and rocks back on his heels.

"Oh, Elijah, that's awful. I'm so sorry," I say, relieved it isn't anything worse. "Did they take anything valuable?"

Elijah scratches the part in his blond hair. "They took my laptop and some of Emma's jewelry that was on top of her dresser. We filed a police report." He shrugs. "They say they'll look into it."

The front door across the street opens, and Emma steps out with a couple kids swirling around her like a flock of geese. Elijah backs away, taking several steps from me and Lissa, in the direction of his own lawn.

"Well, I better head back." Elijah's breezy laughter sounds forced. "Enjoy your lunch."

"Thank you." I offer Elijah a polite smile through tight lips and cast a noncommittal wave to Emma, which she pretends not to see as she skirts to her car with her head down.

I glance at my own house. The break-in does sound worrying. Then a rogue thought enters my mind. What if someone thought Elijah's house was ours? What if it's connected to the viral photo? And then I shrug the thought away.

I head back to the house, with Lissa finally settling in my arms. I'm talking to her softly as we walk in. Then I toss the mail onto the table and place Lissa in her high chair.

Someone coughs.

I spin around, expecting to see Holly returning with the sandwiches. But the room is empty. The cough came from somewhere deeper in the house.

Then I hear footsteps come from upstairs. Elijah hadn't told me what time of day his house had been broken into. Someone may have slipped into the house through the garage door. The fear tangled inside me uncoils into white-hot terror.

Chapter 19

I grab Lissa from her high chair and place her on my hip. With my other hand I scroll through my phone. I'm about to call the police when I remember the secret camera I just installed upstairs. I open the app and view the corridor.

I was right. There is a figure moving along the hallway. My throat catches. I almost scream, but somehow I swallow it.

And then, as quickly as the fear built, it dissipates because I recognize the shape of the figure walking toward the bathroom. I hurry over to the bottom of the stairs.

"Jace?" I call up the steps.

Dead silence greets me from upstairs then the bang of a door slamming.

"Jace! I can hear you. If it's you, answer me. You're scaring me. I thought you were a robber."

This gets him to duck his head around the landing of the stairs.

"What are you doing home from school?" I ask. "Are you sick?" I make a quick assessment of the color in his cheeks and the way he holds himself. He certainly doesn't look sick.

"Umm..." He falters.

As soon as I see the guilt written across his face, I know that ridiculous excuses are about to come pouring from those pale lips. He's caught, a deer trapped in headlights.

"Mom, I... " Jace's frame retreats behind the landing wall, but he keeps his head poked out to gawk down at me. "What are you doing here? Why aren't you at work?"

"I should be asking you the same thing," I tell him. "I have the morning off."

Jace's brow furrows, and he glances past me to the front door. "Where's Holly? Did something happen? Did you have another fight?"

His concerned expression roots me to the floor. He's a twelve-year-old boy. He shouldn't be worrying about arguments at home.

"Why don't you come down here, and we'll talk?" I make my voice sound neutral. It's time for me and Jace to have a proper conversation. And if I want to get any truthful answers out of him, I'm going to have to ease him in.

Jace hesitates but pushes one foot out from behind the wall. His hand travels through his dark hair.

"Am I in trouble?" he asks.

I choose my words carefully. "Let's just talk downstairs, in the kitchen."

The Nanny's Secret

Jace's throat bobs. He inches down the stairs like a worm traveling across a leaf.

I wait for him to get to the bottom, and then I turn around and start walking toward the kitchen. I open the fridge and pluck out a bottle of orange juice before reaching for an apple in the fruit bin. Lissa giggles at the fridge light, and I stroke her cheek before placing her in the high chair. Jace strokes his little sister's hair, his eyes focused intently on Lissa's tiny form. Then he slinks into a chair and stares at me with this guarded expression, as if I'm a bomb about to explode if he doesn't punch in the right code to stop it in time.

The front door opens, and Holly cheerfully shouts out a hello. I quickly get up from the table to greet her before she comes into the kitchen.

I step into the hall. "Hey, Holly." I lower my voice. "Jace is here. He's bunking off school."

"What?" she says, too loudly.

I gesture for her to be quiet. "I'd like to have a chat with him alone, if you don't mind. We should just be a few minutes. Here, I'll take the subs and pop them in the fridge."

"Okay, sure." She hands over a paper bag before making her way up the stairs.

I wait until I hear her bedroom door close, and then I make my way back to Jace. "Holly brought subs, but we didn't know you'd be here so there isn't one for you." The fridge door creaks as I put the sandwiches away.

Jace shrugs. "I'm not hungry anyway."

"Why?" I tilt my head to the side. "Are you sick?"

"No."

"Did you get in trouble at school?"

"No."

"Were you sent home because of some emergency?"

"No."

I slump down in the seat opposite him. "Then why are you *here*, Jace?"

He lifts his eyes to me, and I see his eyebrows knitted with worry. He still cares about getting caught, at least. But instead of coming clean and giving me a true reason why he's skipping school, he shrugs.

"That's it? That's all you are going to do? Shrug at me? You are twelve years old, and you left school without permission. I want to know why."

"I walked home because I didn't feel like being there. I had a headache, and the hallways were too crowded." He brushes his hands up his arms. "I just didn't want to be there."

"Jace, you can't just leave school without telling anyone. It's irresponsible. What if something were to happen to you on the way home? We would have no way to know."

"Mom, we live three blocks away from the school."

"That doesn't matter. There are bad people out there, Jace. You need to stay at school, where you're safe and expected to be." My voice cracks.

"Why do you and Dad keep having these hushed conversations? And why are you so concerned with being safe all of a sudden?" he asks.

I sigh. It's time to come clean. Maybe things will only

The Nanny's Secret

improve between him and me after I'm open and honest with him. "A few weeks ago, someone photoshopped a horrible picture of me doing something... unpleasant. Hurting an animal. It... Well, it went viral, and it has been causing all kinds of problems at work. I've... I've had death threats."

Aside from a red flush working its way up Jace's neck, he doesn't seem surprised. And then it dawns on me. He's already seen it.

"I know," he says. "I just wanted someone to tell me. It's not fair that you leave me out. I'm not a kid, Mom. I understand things."

"Did one of your friends show you the picture?"

"Yeah," he says. "Some of them called you names, but I knew it was fake."

"Jace, I'm so sorry. When you never mentioned it, I thought you must not have seen it. I had no idea."

He shrugs and stares down at his hands. "It's why I came home. I'm sick of it."

"Is there anything I can do?" I ask. "Speak to a teacher—"

"No!" His expression is one of horror. "That would make things ten times worse."

"All right. I won't do that." Then I reach over and squeeze his hand. "You can always talk to me, Jacey."

He shakes his head slightly and looks away. "Why did you take the day off?"

"Well, I wanted to install a security camera."

"It wasn't because you wanted to spend more time with Lissa, was it?" he asks.

"I suppose, partly," I admit. I have been carrying her around a lot this morning.

"Why don't you want to spend time with me too? You could have picked me up from school," he says.

"Well..." I can tell he's fragile in this moment, and I need to tread lightly around his preteen angst. "For starters, I wouldn't assume you'd even *want* to spend time with me. It doesn't seem like you want to be around me lately." I stop at that, not wanting to lay on a guilt trip.

Jace blinks at me, trying to wager how much of what I'm saying is true. "But yet you're willing to spend time with Lissa."

"She's a baby."

"She gets more attention than I do."

"That's *because* she's a baby, and she can't take care of herself," I remind him gently.

"I thought that's what Holly is for." His voice is whining, and I'm actually relieved to hear him sound like a child again.

Jace leans back in his seat. He crosses his arms over his chest.

"It is," I say. I falter, not sure how I can explain everything that has been going on. That I've been feeling insecure about my ability to soothe Lissa, and that's why she's always on my hip. "It's complicated. It's adult stuff."

He scoffs.

"What does that mean?" I ask.

"Probably more lies," he snaps.

I'm surprised by that. I sit up straighter. "Lies?"

"Yeah." He leans forward. "Like you keeping all this

The Nanny's Secret

stuff from me. Adults lie all the time. They tell you what you want to hear to keep the peace, just like what you're doing now. They try to manipulate you so that you'll do what they want. It's all so superficial. It's a double standard. The only adult who doesn't play games, who stays true to who she is on the surface and deep down, is Holly." He angles his eyes away from me and traces the rim of the juice glass with the edge of his finger.

For a moment, I'm speechless. I cannot believe the words coming out of my twelve-year-old son's mouth. Jace has never talked like this before. He's always been a happy-go-lucky kid. It almost sounds as if these judgements have been planted in his mind.

"You— You think Holly is the only adult you can trust?" I gape at him. "You would trust Holly above your own mother and father?"

Jace lifts an eyebrow. "Don't you want me to trust her? You hired her to take care of me and Lissa."

I shake my head, backtracking. "That's— That's not really what I mean."

He sits up straight, his eyes intense. "What do you mean, then?"

"Listen. I am not in the mood to negotiate with my twelve-year-old, so don't try to bait me. You can act smart if you want, but it's not going to get you anywhere with me."

He crosses his arms again and turns his head away from me.

Heat rises up my neck. "For someone who wants freedom, Jace, you are behaving like a spoiled brat. If you don't want to be grounded until college, I would appreciate a little less attitude from you."

He jams a thumbnail in his mouth and starts chewing.

I try a different approach. "Do you consider Holly to be a friend?"

Jace shrugs. "I dunno."

"Would you call her a good friend?"

Jace's cheeks flush pink. "Mom, please."

There is only a thirteen-year age difference between Holly and Jace. They are almost as close in age as Jace is to Lissa. As much as I hate to admit it, this concerns me now that I see the way Jace acts around her or when I'm talking about her. His cheeks stain scarlet if I press him for information about his relationship with her.

"Has Holly told you that she's the only person you can trust?" I ask.

He shakes his head. "She's just cool."

"And you feel like you can talk to her?" I ask.

"Guess so."

"And what about Holly and your dad?" I ask.

Jace's eyes widen in surprise. "What about them?"

I shrug. "Just wondering if you ever notice them hanging out."

"I see them talking sometimes," he admits.

"About what?"

"I don't know. I don't pay that much attention. Mom, you're being even weirder than usual."

"If you heard them talking about anything important, you would tell me, right?" I ask.

The Nanny's Secret

Jace is quiet for a moment. His lips twist, and he scratches at his left cheek.

"There's nothing wrong. Your dad isn't in trouble." I offer a smile. "You are because you skipped school, but not Dad. By the way, I'm taking you back to school after lunch."

Jace's face crumples. "No, Mom, please. Can't we just hang out instead? Please don't make me go back there today."

All the resolve leaves my body when he asks me to hang out. How many years do I have left of Jace wanting to spend time with me?

"All right. Do you want to come to the floral shop this afternoon? I'm setting up more security cameras."

"Sure," he says.

"I'll fix you a sandwich, and you can eat with me and Holly. That okay?"

"Sure," he says.

As I'm grabbing the bread from the cupboard, Jace casually says, "I guess I do see Dad and Holly talking sometimes. She finds him funny."

"He makes her laugh?" I ask.

"Yeah."

With my back turned to Jace, I pull up the app for the security camera and view the footage from the upstairs hall. I almost gasp. Holly is standing right at the top of the stairs, no doubt listening to our conversation.

Chapter 20

There is a change in the way Jace and I interact for the next few days. He happily chatted with Serena in the shop that afternoon as I fitted the security cameras. Then we had a pleasant family meal once Rick came home from work. He went back to school the next day, and we didn't seem to have any issues. I decide to let him attend baseball practice again to reward the change in attitude.

Rick has to visit an important client Friday night, and I'm standing at the kitchen counter, cutting flower stems and bopping along to the radio. Holly is giving Lissa a bath, and Jace is in his room, playing video games. My phone rings, pulling me from my task. At first, I think it's going to be Rick, letting me know he's coming home. But then I frown. Why is Elijah calling me?

Swiping to answer, I give him an apprehensive "Hello?"

He's out of breath and panting, setting me on razor-sharp alarm. "Audrey? Hi. It's Elijah."

"Is everything okay?"

"Well..." He pauses. "Emma has just gone into early labor. We're at the hospital, and she's getting checked in. This is a long shot, and I understand if you can't help at such late notice, but is there any possible way you'd be willing or available to watch the kids for us? It would only be the two littlest ones. They're here at the hospital with us at the moment. It was kind of an emergency, and we had to get going."

"Absolutely. Of course. Whatever you need." I place the stems on the counter and dry my hands with a dish towel. "Give me a couple minutes to get everything together, and I'll pick them up from the hospital."

"You're a lifesaver, Audrey. I won't forget this, trust me."

"It's really no problem."

Holly strides into the kitchen as I'm grabbing my keys from the bowl. "Is everything all right?"

"Well," I say, gripping the door frame while I wiggle one foot into a shoe, "Emma Johnson from across the street went into early labor. Elijah called me from the hospital and asked me if I wouldn't mind picking up Abigail and Axel for them."

I reach for my purse and sling it over my shoulder. "You guys are all good here? Can you let Jace know where I'm going?"

"Yep. No problem."

The expression on Holly's face throws me off guard for

a moment. She seems concerned, but I can't tell why. There's no time to analyze it, however, as I need to get to the hospital. Perhaps I'm projecting my own uncomfortable feelings onto Holly, because I know I have some complicated feelings of my own about the neighbors.

* * *

Elijah is pacing the waiting room when I arrive on the labor and delivery floor. He spins on a heel, his hands tunneling through his hair.

"Audrey, thanks so much for coming. We owe you big time. I'm sorry to throw a wrench in whatever plans you had this evening, but we really do appreciate you coming last minute." Elijah gives me an awkward half hug, half pat on the back.

"How's Emma?" I ask.

"She's hanging in there. She's in a lot of pain and lost a lot of blood." His face pales. "It was a complicated birth."

"What about the baby?"

"A boy." He smiles. "A little premature. But he's a fighter, just like his mama. He's in the NICU right now. I'm going to go see him as soon as you leave with the kids. It's been a difficult few hours. The doctors are monitoring her. I just want to spend as much time with our little tiebreaker as I can."

It doesn't escape me that Elijah is a lot more excited for his son than he's concerned for his wife.

"Will they both be okay?" I ask.

"They have to be. I won't have it any other way. I need

The Nanny's Secret

my team, you know? My Emma and my little boy. My poor boy. He's hooked up to all these monitors and tubes."

"I'm so sorry. Rick and I will help in any way we can. We can keep Axel and Abigail for as long as you need."

"Thank you so much." Elijah blows out a relieved breath and walks toward his kids, scooping them off the floor, explaining to them that they are going home with me while their mommy and new brother rest. "The older kids caught a bus to my parents' house. We've had to shuffle them around as best we can. Emma's parents are going to call at yours tomorrow and pick them up for the weekend. But they wanted to be at the hospital tonight."

"Sure," I say, understanding that Emma probably wanted her mom with her.

The two blond-haired kids gaze up at me with their father's eyes. I lean down and try to reassure them that everything will be okay. Then they lace their fingers through mine, and I lead them down to the parking lot. Both children are quiet, but I'm sure they're picking up on all the stress in the atmosphere right now.

After I load the kids into the car, my thoughts are heavy on the drive home. I can't stop picturing Emma's little baby hooked up to machines. And I can't stop thinking about how distraught Emma probably is, in a fragile condition herself, unable to hold and bond with her new baby. I remember her last birth being a difficult one too. Sometimes I wonder if Elijah sees her as a baby-making machine and ties in her worth with her ability to have children.

Once we're home, Holly helps me get Abigail and Axel settled. Abigail is six, and she loves to play with Lissa's doll, pretending it's her baby. It's a nice distraction. Axel, who is three, asks about his mommy and when she'll come get him. I try my best to comfort him and tell him that his mommy just had a baby and needs to stay at the hospital for a little while, but his daddy will come get him soon. He seems satisfied with that answer, and after Holly makes him a snack of cheese and crackers, he starts to warm up to us.

I sit down on the couch, watching Holly supervise Abigail and Axel. We're letting them wind down before we put them to bed. There are two small mattresses set up in Holly's room for the night.

While the kids are busy with a set of blocks on the floor, Holly glances at me. "You look worried."

I pick at my thumbnail. "I am."

"Do you want to talk about it?"

I tuck my feet under my legs and shrug. "I'm just thinking about poor Emma. She's gone through so much. First they're robbed, and now a second complicated birth for her. I hope she'll be okay and recover fast. Elijah mentioned at the hospital that she had lost a lot of blood and that the baby was in the NICU, hooked up to monitors."

Holly's expression is impassive. Like a blank canvas. It makes me feel as though she's holding something back. "I hope they're both okay."

She turns away from me and helps Axel build a tower out of blocks. She gets quiet after that, not asking any more questions about Emma, the new baby, or otherwise. She doesn't look at me again, avoiding my gaze. It's as if she'd

The Nanny's Secret

rather slink into the cracks of the floorboards than talk to me about Emma and the baby.

Axel smacks his hand against the tower of blocks that Holly had stacked to purposely make it fall. One of the blocks goes flying and hits Holly on the side of her face.

"I'm sorry," Axel says, on the brink of tears.

I stroke his hair. "It's all right. It was only an accident. Look. Holly is fine now."

"He still needs to learn to be careful," Holly snaps.

I turn to her, bemused. "Holly, come on. He's only three."

"You're right," she says. "Sorry. It's just a lot with... with two kids. Maybe we should put them to bed now."

"I'll help you."

Holly nods and seems genuinely grateful.

I suppose it is more stressful looking after two children, but I've never seen her snap at Lissa or Jace. For all of the issues I've had with Holly, I've never once suspected her of being harsh on the kids. If anything, she's a little too sweet at times. It's odd to me that she looks at Axel and Abigail completely differently than Lissa. And I can't help but wonder why.

Chapter 21

At some point in the middle of the night, Rick slips into bed, and I tell him all about Emma Johnson and the two children in Holly's room. I smell beer on his breath, which might explain why he didn't answer his phone when I tried to tell him about the Johnsons earlier.

It's not unusual for Rick's company to wine and dine a client. But I can't help but feel a tiny bit resentful, given the stressful day I've had.

"I have that conference this weekend," he says. "Are you going to be okay if I go? It's just that it's been booked for—"

"We'll be fine." I turn away from him and try to sleep.

Rick's hand lingers on my hip, but then it slides away, and I hear him start to snore.

It's not as though I want him to stay just because I'm babysitting the neighbors' kids, but at the same time, I wish he was around more so that I feel less alone in all

The Nanny's Secret

this. But the middle of the night isn't the time to start an argument.

The doorbell chimes early on Saturday morning as I'm pouring my first cup of coffee. Rick has already left. Axel and Abigail just had a quick breakfast of cereal, and Holly is changing Lissa's diaper upstairs.

I shuffle through the hall in slippers to see two silhouettes on the other side of the frosted glass of the door. Emma's parents.

"Morning," I say brightly, swinging the door open. "Sorry about not being dressed yet." I gesture to my robe.

"Oh, we're just happy you took the kids in," the woman says. "I'm Karen, and this is Stephen."

"Come in," I say, gesturing for them to follow me. "I just made coffee if you'd like some."

"I think I'll take that coffee, thank you," Karen says.

I notice that Emma favors her mother in looks. Her straight, light-blond hair has a few strands of gray that catch in the morning sunlight spilling in from the kitchen windows.

Abigail and Axel both hop down from the breakfast bar as soon as their grandparents walk in. Both Karen and Stephen open their arms and scoop a kid into each.

Axel blinks up at his grandma and asks, "Where's Mommy, Nana?"

"She's resting after having the baby, sweetheart." Karen kisses Axel's head and strokes his hair.

Stephen gestures to an overnight bag. "I have a change of clothes here. Can I take them somewhere to get dressed?"

"Sure." I quickly show Stephen where the living room is and then join Karen back in the kitchen.

"How is Emma doing?" I busy myself with pouring two cups of coffee.

"It was a hard night," Karen says. "She's doing a lot better this morning, but she's going to have to be in the hospital a few more days." She lets out a long breath, and I see the stress of the last day etched on her face.

I push one cup over to her. "What about the baby?"

"He's still in the NICU, but he's strong, and they say he'll be off the oxygen and breathing on his own by early next week."

"That's good news, at least." I take a sip of my drink.

Emma's mother wraps her hands around the mug and glances down at the dark liquid. "I'm so glad they'll both pull through. Oh, poor Emma. I asked her if four was enough children. The last birth was almost as bad." She sighs.

Just at that moment, Stephen walks back in without the kids. "Karen, it's her choice."

I can tell Karen has more to say. But a moment later, the kids barrel into the room with their backpacks slung over their tiny shoulders.

"We're ready for pancakes, Nana!" Axel exclaims.

I walk them to the door while Emma's parents thank me for keeping the two youngest. As I say goodbye and close the front door behind me, I can't help but wonder what Karen was about to say in the kitchen. But I've had my fill of dealing with the Johnsons.

The Nanny's Secret

"We should do something fun today. You, me, and Jace."

I turn around to find Holly walking down the stairs, carrying Lissa.

I give her a quizzical look. "Like what?"

Holly shrugs. She looks fresh with no makeup, her hair pulled up in a ponytail. She's wearing a baggy T-shirt and pajama pants.

"Maybe we could go to lunch at that new bar and grill downtown? Just to get out of the house?"

"Sure, that sounds great, Holly. Thanks for suggesting it. Then I can check in at the shop with Serena while we're down there."

Holly's eyes crinkle as she smiles. "Great."

I'm optimistic. Maybe this will shape up to be a good day.

* * *

Jace orders a burger and fries, scarfing it down while he plays a video game on his phone. Holly feeds Lissa from a restaurant high chair while she takes bites from her chicken sandwich.

"So, how's Emma doing?" Holly asks.

I lean back in my chair and give Holly a quick update.

"So how long will she be in the hospital?" Holly asks.

"They didn't give specifics." I stab a piece of lettuce with the prong of my fork and chew it.

"Like a few days?" Holly's eyes are steady on mine now.

"Probably."

I frown, wondering why Holly cares so much about Emma's hospital stay. It seems more than simple curiosity.

A few things about Holly have stood out recently. I caught her listening to my conversation with Jace. While that doesn't necessarily mean she has a nefarious scheme up her sleeve, it does suggest that she's at least nosy. And then she snapped at Axel, which seemed out of character. Now she seems oddly interested in Emma's whereabouts.

Holly grabs a baby wipe to clean off Lissa's face. "So is Emma going to make a full recovery?"

"I honestly don't know much else," I admit. "Her mother seemed pretty stressed about it all."

"But her baby's all right?" Emma's eyebrows rise. "It was a boy?"

"Yes, a boy. He's in the NICU, but I hear he's doing well."

"That's good." Holly's mouth twists, as if she's concentrating on working something out in her head.

"Can we stop talking about the goddamn Johnsons, please," Jace says, throwing down a fork.

My jaw almost drops. "Jace! Language!"

He picks up his fork and spears a fry.

"What was that outburst for?" I ask.

Jace shrugs. But before I can continue questioning him, Lissa smears apricot paste on her bib and distracts me. I wonder if this is about Jace lacking attention again. Maybe the two younger kids coming into the house on short notice threw him off-kilter. So I decide to go easy on him, and we finish the rest of our lunch without incident.

The Nanny's Secret

Holly and I get the kids into the car, and we head home. Even though the last few days have been busy, it's been good to take my mind off the death threats. I haven't even checked my email. But at least with the security cameras on the house and at the shop, I have a weight off my shoulders.

There are just tiny things bothering me about Holly now. Even though I wonder why she cares so much about Emma and why she listened in on our conversation, the more time goes on, the less I suspect her of trying to sabotage my business. Surely something else would have happened by now.

I ease into the drive home. One good thing about Rick being away is that we can order takeout tonight and slob around. Maybe Holly and I can put on a chick flick. Jace will be upstairs playing games anyway.

And then something happens to ruin my day. Elijah is sitting on the brick steps leading up to my front porch. He's holding a bottle wrapped in a brown paper bag. His body is swaying, and his eyes are half-open. His hair is sticking up in the back.

Jace sits up straight in his seat and peers at Elijah out the car window.

"Is there something wrong with Mr. Johnson?"

Holly stiffens in the passenger seat beside me and gives me a guarded look.

I park in the garage, not answering Jace right away because I'm stunned to find Elijah on my front steps.

"Jace, why don't you help Holly take the to-go boxes into the house while I go check on Mr. Johnson?"

As they do what I asked, I grab my purse and stride over to the front of the house. My stomach twists into tight knots. Then I stop six feet away from Elijah. His eyelids are drooping, and the bottle slips from his lazy grip.

"Elijah?" I ask, albeit reluctantly. "Is everything all right?"

He lets out a half snort, half huff. I wince and take a step back. He reeks of booze. His skin is clammy and his hair damp and matted to his temples and the back of his neck. His skin is the color of raw chicken.

I try again. "Elijah, why are you here? How much have you had to drink? Is Emma okay? The baby?"

"Whoa, whoa, whoa," he yammers. "What's with the third degree? You're not my wife. I don't have to answer to you."

"Yes, but you are on my property, Elijah."

He frowns and glances around as if he's confused. "I am?"

"Yes. And you appear to be drunk. Tell me what happened and why you're here."

He opens his mouth to speak but clamps it shut a moment later.

"What's wrong, Elijah?"

He's silent.

"Tell me what happened."

His half-closed eyes regard me with utter hatred. My heart drops out of my chest.

Chapter 22
HOLLY

I wait until Jace is upstairs, and then I put Lissa in her Pack 'n Play with a few toys to keep her busy. Hopefully it will bide me a few minutes, at least.

I'm on my way to the garage when the light in the living room catches my eye. The bulb is different. It's larger, and the glass is a different color. At first, I don't know why I'm noticing it. Or why the hairs stand up on the back of my neck.

It just seems odd that I never noticed Rick or Audrey change the lightbulb. And I certainly never saw the bulb blow.

I shake the thought away and move quickly and quietly toward the garage. I toss my purse back in the car. If Audrey finds me out here, I can pretend I've come to collect it. Then I pad to the front of the garage and slip one foot out onto the pavement, craning my neck around the side of the house. My heart hammers violently against my ribcage as I eavesdrop on Audrey's private conversation with Rick.

"Tell me what's really going on, Elijah." Audrey sounds equal parts irritated and alarmed. I've noticed the change in her around Elijah. She's constantly on edge, and I'm pretty sure I know why.

Elijah doesn't answer right away. He chokes out a half sob, half croak. "Emma had to have an emergency hysterectomy right after the delivery."

Audrey gasps. "Oh, Elijah, I'm so sorry. Is she okay?"

"Her uterus ruptured during the delivery." He swigs his liquor.

"But thank God she survived," Audrey says. "And your new baby boy."

When Elijah answers, his voice is so cold, goose bumps travel across my skin. "She won't be able to get pregnant again without a uterus."

The air around me stagnates, and for a solid thirty seconds, not a word is spoken between them. My stomach lurches. For a heartbeat or longer, I think I might actually be sick.

Finally, Audrey breaks the silence, and her voice is low and angry. "What the fuck, Elijah? I... I can't believe you just said that about your wife as she recovers in the hospital. What is she, a brood mare to you? Why are you here, sitting on my porch, getting drunk, when you should be at the hospital as a moral support for her and to comfort her? I'm sure she's just as devastated as you are."

"You don't think I know that?" Elijah barks back then

The Nanny's Secret

sighs. "I just... I just needed a break. I just needed some air." His voice cracks.

"Do you want me to take you back to the hospital?" Audrey forces the words out, as if doing that is the last thing on earth she wants to do but feels an obligation to suggest it anyway. "I can get you some coffee to sober you up."

"No, I'm going home to sleep it off."

"Maybe that's best, then." Audrey folds her arms, and I can tell she just wants to get rid of this drunken man. "I'm sure everything will be fine. She just needs to recover, and then she'll be back to normal. The nurses and doctors are doing everything they can to help her and the baby."

Elijah coughs. "Yeah."

Elijah stands up and stretches his arms to the sky, clutching the paper bag with the bottle in his hand.

"Sorry to ruin your afternoon with all my drama." He grins now, like he's trying to be charming.

Audrey frowns and drags a toe across a patch of gravel. "Don't worry about it. I'll be thinking about and praying for your family."

Elijah scoffs and staggers down the sidewalk leading to the driveway. "Sure you will."

Audrey looks at him for a moment with pity glazing her eyes. She shakes her head and clomps back into her house, the door slamming in her wake.

As soon as she's gone, I decide to take another chance. I step out of the garage and head around a large bush next to the driveway. Timing my exit perfectly for when Elijah reaches the sidewalk, I step out and pretend as though I'm coming from the opposite direction.

"Hi, Elijah. Is everything okay?" I ask sweetly.

He gives me an indifferent wave.

"How's Emma?" I clear my throat, crossing my arms over my chest. "And the baby?"

He shakes his head slightly. "She's doing better, but it's going to be a long road. She had to have a hysterectomy."

"I'm so sorry."

His eyes meet mine, and he places a hand on my arm. His fingers are warm and slick. "Thanks for your concern." And then he narrows his eyes slightly. "You have a nice face, you know. A calm face."

"Thanks—"

"I bet you're good under pressure. Real steady. And you'll make a good mom someday. I see you with the baby. It's cute." He smiles.

"Thanks."

"A very nice face," he mumbles. "You look so familiar to me. I've been trying to figure it out. I'm sure I know you from somewhere."

"You've met me before. I was at your barbeque."

Elijah's blue eyes turn overcast. "No, that's not it. I know you from somewhere else. I'm sure of it."

I had hoped to keep him talking awhile longer and maybe get some information out of him about Audrey, but this conversation is taking a turn I don't like. I back away.

"I'd better go help Audrey with the kids," I say.

"You're a good girl, ain't ya?" He grins. "One of these

The Nanny's Secret

days, we'll have a sit-down and a chat. I'll help you with your finances, if you like."

"Sure." I take another step back. "Please give my best wishes to your wife."

I turn around, my body trembling. And then I see Audrey watching me from the window.

Shit.

Chapter 23

Why would Holly go over to Elijah and talk to him? Holly doesn't know Elijah, and I've already told her how Emma is. Elijah is currently drunk and volatile. So why would a young woman go out of her way to speak to this man? It doesn't make any sense.

I move away from the window, but I'm sure that Holly has seen me. I make my way into the kitchen and start unloading the dishwasher so that I can appear to be nonchalant when Holly walks back into the house.

She enters through the garage door with her purse in hand. "I left it in the car." She smiles.

"And then went to talk to Elijah?" I ask.

She adjusts the strap of her bag on her shoulder and avoids my eye contact. "He saw me and waved me over." She clears her throat. "He was asking me about whether I could take on a second position to help him and his wife with their kids. But I said no, that I was full time with you."

The Nanny's Secret

"Oh, I see," I say. "I suppose that's understandable given everything that's going on with Emma and the baby."

She nods. "I'll go and check on Lissa. I put her in her Pack 'n Play before grabbing my purse."

I watch Holly leave. I know she's lying. I saw her approach Elijah, not the other way around, and I doubt very much that he tried to poach my nanny. Elijah is not the kind of man to allow his wife help with the kids. He's the kind of man to demand traditional roles, no matter how hard things are for Emma. He would probably have Emma's mother move in to help rather than hire out.

But why would Holly lie?

* * *

"Audrey!" Emma tries to sit up too quickly and winces. "What are you doing here?"

"Please, don't get up," I tell her, entering the room. "I'm on my lunch break at work, and I just thought I'd pop in to see how you're doing since the hospital is so close by."

A flush of color returns to Emma's wan face. She looks exhausted. Her cheeks are hollow, and she has dark circles under her eyes. She still has an IV port on the top of her hand. My eyes wander to the plexiglass hospital bassinet beside her. The baby is sleeping, a tiny blue hat on his round head. He's swaddled in a pastel-colored hospital blanket. I peer down at his pink cheeks and puckered mouth. His eyelids are closed, eyes moving beneath them. His chest rises and falls peacefully.

"He's beautiful, Emma."

"Thanks." Her voice catches. "He officially left the NICU this morning. He'll need special pediatric care for a couple weeks, but he's strong and breathing on his own now."

"I forgot how tiny preemie babies are." I take a step toward him, and my chest tightens. He's so small. I can't help but think of everything Emma went through.

"We named him Zander," Emma says.

I look up at her. "No name that starts with A?"

Emma puts on a brave face, but her chin wobbles.

"Elijah wanted to go with a Z name this time because we won't be able to have any more children. He said we might as well have A to Z and close it out."

I shake my head. "I'm sorry, Emma, but that's cruel. I —" I snap my mouth shut with a click. "Sorry. But I don't like the way he's treating you."

She sniffles, and a single tear rolls down her cheek, landing on her hospital gown. "He won't want to be with me anymore."

"Oh, Emma." I step forward and cup a hand over hers. "Do you want to be with him? After everything?"

Her eyes darken. "He's my husband."

I don't know what to say. If she can't see how terrible he is, then I don't know what I can say to convince her.

Zander stirs in the bassinet. Emma stiffens and reaches to pull it closer to her.

"Can I hold him?" I ask before she can lift him out.

"Of course." She shrugs.

I lift him gently and sit down on the gray chair beside

The Nanny's Secret

Emma. The cushions are stiff, like sitting on wooden boards, but I settle into it and cradle Zander close to my chest. He yawns, his eyes fluttering.

I pull the top of his hat off his head, and underneath, a tuft of dark-blond hair juts out. I brush my fingers through the soft strands. There's an unsettled sensation churning through my stomach, a pang throbbing through my heart that I can't identify.

"Where is Elijah? Will he be back soon?" I ask.

"I have no idea where he is," she replies.

I stand up and carefully place Zander back in his bassinet.

Emma adjusts slightly so she can check over her newborn. But as she moves, she sucks in a sharp breath. "Ouch."

"Do you want me to get the nurse?"

She shakes her head.

I disobey her and click the button for assistance. "I'm so sorry, but I need to go. I'll wait until the nurse gets here."

"Thanks for coming to visit me and Zander. It's been... lonely in here." The smile she gives me does not reach her exhausted eyes.

Anger heats my cheeks. Her husband should be here, helping her. Instead he's moping around, drinking himself into a hole because he can't father any more kids.

"Zander is absolutely beautiful." The sentiment sounds weak and watered down, but it's the best I can do. I have the sudden urge to bolt from this room, to leave the uncomfortable sadness behind me.

"Thank you," she says.

I turn to leave, glancing back at her once to cast her a wave, but she's not looking at me. She's gazing down at her newborn son as if it's only them against the big, cruel world on the other side of these four walls.

Chapter 24

"Um, Audrey?"

I hear Serena's voice, but it doesn't register that she's standing right in front of me until she wiggles her fingers a few inches from my face.

I blink the glaze from my eyes. "Yes?"

My pen hovers above the order I'm ready to process.

"It's a dozen roses for that order." Serena points at the error I've written in the description box. "Not two dozen."

"Oh my goodness." I press a palm to my forehead. "Thank you, Serena. That's a good save."

I need to snap out of this daze I've been in ever since leaving the hospital. Something about that visit with Emma isn't sitting right with me.

"And those bouquets are supposed to have personalized notes attached with them," Serena says gently. She picks up one of the orders going out for delivery by the end of the day. "They don't have envelopes with them yet, unless you just hadn't gotten to that point and want me to take care of it."

I shake my head slightly. "Right. You're right. Wow, I am away with the fairies right now!"

"Is everything okay?" Serena tilts her head to one side, her eyes slightly narrowed. "Have you had any more threatening emails, anything like that?"

"No. Actually, that seems to have ended. Finally. I never heard back from the police, though. I guess they didn't get the IP address after all." My skin crawls at the thought of someone out there living their lives as though nothing happened. Meanwhile, I'm constantly checking the video feeds on my phone, paranoid someone will try to break into my store or home. And my insurance has skyrocketed since we made a claim.

"I don't know what's wrong with me. I should be feeling back to my old self." I shake my head.

Serena gives my arm a squeeze. "Hey, no one is one hundred percent all the time. We all have our bad days, or days where we feel more *off* than normal."

"What's a normal amount of bad and off days?" I try to joke. "Because it seems like I've had a lot of them back-to-back."

Serena takes a step away from me, on her way back to the store front. "You are a kick-ass businesswoman who built this place from the ground up. I admire your strength. You have a lot of shining qualities that you don't always see in yourself, but they exist, if you're willing to look. Right?"

I laugh. "Right."

The Nanny's Secret

It's what I needed to hear after Rick threw my confidence the other week.

A smile tugs at the corners of her lips. "I'm going to give the shop a sweep real quick. You okay at the register?"

"Sure."

Foot traffic has been steadily improving since the viral picture incident. A two-for-one on lily bouquets helps too. I serve an elderly man buying flowers for his wife and a woman who wants a bouquet of daisies for her mother. Then I put together an order for a funeral. It's a busy day, and I'm slowly disengaging from the entanglement I feel with the Johnsons. I'm gradually erasing the image of tiny Zander Johnson in my arms.

But the moment I walk out into the parking lot, I notice something different about my car. It's like it's leaning too much to the right. Did I accidentally park on the curb, and that's what's causing it to look unlevel?

I walk closer to inspect it and notice both of my right tires are flat. They're deflated all the way to the rim. I kneel down and grumble a few choice swear words, craning my neck around and brushing my fingertips across the tread, trying to locate the source. One tire I could replace, but two?

My fingertip finds a gaping hole at the top of the back tire.

"Are you fucking kidding me?"

Someone has slashed my tires.

The timing is just perfect. After daring to inform the universe I haven't been targeted for a while, I end up being targeted yet again. I rock back on my heels, dragging my fingers through my hair.

Then I open the app on my phone. I have a security camera on the back of the shop now. The app sends me a notification when there's an event, but it usually turns out to be a raccoon searching for trash or someone walking by on the road. Quickly, I scan through the events. There's one notification telling me that the connection with the device has been lost.

"What the hell?" I mumble.

The event before the disabled connection takes me by surprise. In the distance, there's a shape. A person standing just off to the left, barely out of sight. They raise their arm and toss an object at the camera. I flinch back as the object —a rock, I think—smashes the camera.

I replay it, trying to glean as much information from that two-second glimpse of the person as I can. Is it a man or a woman? Are they tall? Short? But it's surprisingly difficult to tell when everything happens so quickly and the person is wearing a shapeless black outfit and a ski mask.

Then I save the footage to my phone and call Detective Stalks. He answers quickly, and I relay everything to him. I send him the video footage.

"Can you sit tight in the store?" he asks. "I can be there to take a formal statement in about thirty minutes."

"Sure," I say, my stomach squirming.

I turn back from the car, with the image of my stalker burned into my brain. The ski mask. The lumpy shape of him or her. Was it a man? My instinct says yes. The height and weight, even in that brief, blurry glimpse, felt like a man. Then I check my watch. Rick said he would be leaving the conference about now. He's probably driving.

As I open the door back into the shop, I try his number, but it goes straight to voice mail.

"Hey," Serena calls. "I thought you were leaving."

"Someone slashed my tires."

"Fuck. Seriously? Are you okay?"

I nod. "A detective is coming out in thirty minutes. Look at this."

Serena leans over my shoulder in the back of the shop as I replay her the footage. She winces away from the flying rock in the same way I did.

"Whoever it is doesn't want to get caught," she says. "That's it. I'm staying with you until the police arrives."

"You don't have to—"

"No arguments," she says. "Shit. I biked to work today. Otherwise I could take you home later. Maybe the police can."

I don't like the idea of Serena biking home alone either. "Maybe he can take us both."

We lock the front and back doors to the floral shop, make sure the closed sign is on, and then wait in my office.

"I'm so sorry, Aud," Serena says. "You don't deserve any of this stuff happening to you."

I grab her hand. "I hate that it's affecting the shop. Rick..." I pull in a deep breath, trying not to allow myself to cry. "Rick said I'll have to sell if business doesn't improve. I'm so sorry that this might affect you too."

"Hey," she says. "None of this is your fault. Some

psycho is targeting you because they're jealous or bored or sad, and there's nothing you can do about it."

I wipe away the tears escaping from my eyes and steady my breath. "I should call the nanny and let her know I'll be home late."

"All right. I'll go check the shop again," she says.

I call as soon as Serena steps out of the office, but Holly's phone also goes to voice mail. And then I think to myself that this is the final straw. If she doesn't call back within the next thirty minutes, she's fired. Though I don't say that as I leave a message.

No, I don't think this was Holly. The person throwing the rock seemed substantially taller and stronger.

Unless she had help.

I call Jace's phone. It's switched off.

Every hair on the back of my neck stands on end. Something is wrong.

Chapter 25

It's my first time meeting Detective Stalks, and he's younger than I expected. A set of straight white teeth peeks out from his full lips when he smiles. Next to me, Serena's spine straightens.

"How are you holding up, Mrs. Miller?" he asks, shaking my hand.

"Actually, not great," I admit. "I'm sure it's nothing, but I can't get hold of my nanny or son."

He frowns slightly. "Do you feel that's a cause for concern?"

"Considering someone slashed my tires today, I'd say so." I run a trembling hand through my hair. "My nanny is a little... Well, she's done this before. She let her phone run out of charge. And my son can also be forgetful."

He smiles. "I'm sure that's it. But if you like, I can have an officer stop by the house."

"That would be great," I say.

"Deep breaths," Serena reminds me as the detective steps away to make a phone call.

"At least they're taking this seriously." I let out a long, slow breath, taking Serena's advice.

After the detective arranges a house call, we head out into the parking lot, and he examines the tires. He then looks at the camera and checks the video footage again. He also checks the video footage for the front door in case the stalker happened to walk past. But we don't see anyone in similar clothes.

"Okay," the detective says, rocking back on his heels, "this is what I'm going to do. I'll have a couple officers ask around the businesses in the area. We can pull CCTV from the area and check for anyone matching the description of the man on your video."

"So you think it's a man?" I ask.

He waves a hand in the air as though weighing the evidence. "I'd say so from the shape we saw, but I'm also not ruling out that it could be a woman." He puts his hands in his pockets. "Now, I'm not going to lie, tire slashing is not a huge priority. But I don't like the way this is escalating. From the viral image, to the threats you received, and now this physical presence. Please be reassured, Mrs. Miller, we are taking this seriously."

His phone rings, and he lifts a finger to tell me to wait a moment. Then he steps into my office to take the call.

"At least they're taking it seriously," Serena says.

I nod. There is that. I've heard horror stories about women murdered by their stalkers because the police failed to do anything.

The Nanny's Secret

The detective strides back into the storefront, where I'm waiting with Serena. "I just heard from the colleague checking your house. He knocked on the door and said there wasn't an answer."

I place a hand on my thumping heart. "There wasn't?"

He shakes his head. "But like you said, it might be because the nanny took the kids out for a walk. It's a lovely evening."

I shake my head slightly. "I don't know. I suppose it's possible, but Holly should be giving Lissa her dinner by now. Something's wrong. I know it is."

* * *

Detective Stalks offers to drive me home. He drops Serena off at her house first as it's on the way. I can tell she doesn't want to leave me, but I assure her that I'll call her as soon as I know everything will be okay.

We're practically silent on the rest of the journey to my place. Ten minutes feel like hours. The car slows to a crawl along our drive. The house is in darkness, with the blinds and drapes drawn shut. No lights are on in the windows or on the porch. It is a haunted reflection of my life.

But Holly's car is still in the driveway, which is strange. Would she take the kids out without her car? Perhaps, as the detective said, she took them for a walk. But even still, she should be back by now as it's getting dark.

"Okay, Mrs. Miller. I'm going to come in with you and sweep the house. Then we'll try to locate the nanny. When does your husband get home?"

"He's on his way back from a conference. I... I haven't been able to get through to him, but he never answers the phone when he's driving. It could be another two or three hours before he's home." My voice is shaking. I've never wanted Rick here with me so much in my entire life. Being here, alone, trying to make the right decisions for my family is complete and utter hell.

"All right," he says. "Let's go in, shall we? Try to stay calm. In these cases, the most likely scenario is that someone has left their phone behind."

I nod and unclip the seat belt. I feel like I'm walking through molasses on my way to the door. I fumble with my keys and unlock the deadbolt, switching on the light in the darkened foyer.

"Hello? Anyone home?"

Silence is the only thing in the house to greet us. I glance behind me at the detective. He steps in front of me and pulls a gun from the holster beneath his jacket. The sight of it makes my stomach flip.

"Jace?" I call.

Stalks nods to me and makes his way up the stairs.

I clasp my hands tightly together until they're tangled in a knot. My son. My daughter. Both not at home where they should be. Deep down inside all I can think about is how all of this is my fault. One way or the other, I allowed evil into my home. I put my trust in a place it should never have been.

With the detective in front, we check the rooms upstairs and then downstairs. The house is empty. I half collapse onto a dining table, and Stalks opens each of the

The Nanny's Secret

cupboard doors until he finds a glass. He fills it with water and hands it to me.

"How about trying the nanny again," he suggests.

I'm reaching for my phone when I hear a key in the door. And then I'm on my feet rushing through the hall. Stalks is behind me somewhere, trying to keep up. The door swings open, and my breath catches in my throat.

"Mom? What are you doing here?"

I rush forward and scoop my twelve-year-old kid into my arms, smooshing him so hard that he physically recoils.

"Jace! Where have you been?"

He pulls out of my grip and stares up at me.

"It's past dinner time," I say. "Where are Holly and Lissa?"

Jace licks his lips and glances to the left as though searching for an answer. "I was at Alec's house."

"This whole time?" I ask.

"Since after school." He lifts his gaze.

"Why didn't you answer your phone?"

For the first time, Jace notices Detective Stalks, and his eyes widen. Then they turn to me and flare. "Mom. Who is that? Where's Dad? What's going on?"

I'm surprised by the anger in his eyes. I don't answer for a moment, and in that split second, Jace's expression turns livid.

"You're such a liar, Mom! I hate you."

He tries to push past me, but I grasp hold of his arms.

"Jace, what are you talking about? This is Detective Stalks. He's here because someone slashed my tires."

His face pales. When I let go of his arms, he takes an uneasy step back and whispers, "Oh."

"Nice to meet you, Jace." The detective reaches out a hand. "Sorry to scare you. I know it's a bit worrying to see a strange man in the house. But you're doing a good job at keeping your mom safe. Good instincts there."

I'm appreciative of the detective for breezing past Jace's weird accusation. I stare at him. The little boy with the baby cheeks and the vibrant smile is long gone. His expression is pulled tight with anxiety. It's like he's carrying the weight of something. A secret, perhaps.

I do something I haven't done for years. I crouch down like he's a child. Only this time I'm looking up at him. "Jace, this is very important. I don't know where Holly is, and she has Lissa with her. If you know where Holly is, you need to tell me."

Jace avoids my gaze and stares above my head. "I don't know where she is."

"Are you lying?" I resist the urge to grab hold of his chin and make him look at me.

He lowers his head, his expression wounded. "Why would I lie about that?"

"So you're telling me that you don't know where your nanny is? Did you tell her where you would be? Or is she out looking for you, and that's why she isn't here?"

Jace scratches the back of his neck. "She's not out looking for me."

"Well, she's not answering the phone." I try a gentler approach. "I'm just trying to get in touch with her. If you know anything, now is the time to say it."

The Nanny's Secret

Jace shakes his head. "I don't know where she is. I..."

I stand up straight. "What, Jace?" I sense the detective behind me, taking in all this family drama. If I wasn't so panicked, I'd be embarrassed.

"She might have sent me a message earlier, but my phone ran out of battery before I could open it," he says.

I sense that there's more to it. "Let's charge your phone then. Go and plug it in." As Jace runs up the stairs, I turn to the detective. "I don't like this. I think the nanny has taken my baby."

"Do you want to report your baby missing?" he asks.

"Yes," I say. "I do."

Chapter 26

Stalks insists that I take a moment to sit and drink some water. He's clearly concerned that I'm losing it. I sip the water and answer some basic questions about Lissa. He takes a photo of a picture of Lissa and Holly together.

"I've now got officers out there looking for them," Stalks says. "Shall we check your son's phone?"

I nod and call Jace down from his bedroom. When I lock eyes with him, a pit of dread opens in my stomach. With everything going on, I'm not sure I'm able to pull at the thread coiled inside my body, but I know Jace is keeping a secret from me. A huge one.

"Here," Jace says, handing me his phone.

I scan two messages. The first one reads, *Hey, Jace. Are you going to Alec's after school? Have a great time.*

The second one makes the hairs stand up on the back of my neck.

You're a great kid, Jace. Tell your mom I'm sorry.

The Nanny's Secret

My hand flies up to my mouth. This confirms it. There's no other way of reading this message, given the facts of the situation. Holly has stolen my child. Detective Stalks frowns down at the message.

"Are you sure you didn't read this message?" I ask Jace.

He shakes his head. His cheeks bloom a bright red.

"You did, didn't you? Why didn't you say right away? Are you still trying to protect her?"

"No." But he starts to cry. "Okay, I saw it, and I ran home. I thought I might be able to find her first because I knew you'd get mad."

I am mad. I'm so livid I could smack my son around the face. But I don't. Instead I grab the glass of water and launch it across the room, watching as glass explodes against the wall.

"She has *Lissa*. Your baby sister. Don't you understand that? Don't you know what's going on?"

Out of the corner of my eye, I notice the detective step out of the room to take a phone call.

"Mom, I'm sorry!" He's crying harder. "I've messed up so bad."

I stare at him a moment longer, and it's like a jigsaw puzzle piece just slid into place. But before I can say anything, Stalks returns.

"One of our officers has a lead. Do you know a neighbor called Elijah Johnson?"

My scalp tingles. "Yes."

"He saw Holly pushing a stroller a few blocks away. I have a patrol car out looking for her."

I rush past the detective into the hallway.

"Mrs. Miller, I think it would be best if you stayed here," he says.

I shake my head. "No, I have to go. I can't just wait around here."

"I'm coming with you, Mom." Jace catches up to me by the door.

I grab my keys from the bowl.

"How about I come with you both," the detective suggests. "That way I can drive."

***

"Mom," Jace says from the back of the car. "Why would Holly leave the neighborhood?"

At this point, we've been around the neighborhood twice and checked all the parks within a few miles. Stalks has turned the car around, and we're on our way back to the house.

"I don't know." Even I can hear the note of defeat in my voice. I glance at Jace in the rearview mirror. "Is there anything else you're not telling me?"

"I don't know..." He trails off, his hands dragging through his hair. "I don't know. She wouldn't. I know she wouldn't."

"Wouldn't what?" I say.

Jace shakes his head.

I know what he's trying to say. That she wouldn't take my child. But I can't think of any other explanation than the one we have here. Holly is gone, and so is my baby.

"I think it's time for you to wake up, Jace. Holly was

The Nanny's Secret

never your friend. She had an agenda this entire time." I shake my head, wondering how unhinged a person needs to be in order to steal a baby. I think I'm going to be sick.

Stalks's car pulls up to the drive. "Guys, I need to drop you off here. I'm going to send an officer to your house to make sure you're doing all right. But my work continues at the station now. I need to coordinate with my team to find your daughter. Okay, Mrs. Miller?"

I nod. My entire body is numb. I can't believe this is happening, that I'm having these conversations.

"Mom, I don't like this," Jace says. I can tell the realization of it all keeps hitting him in waves.

"Thank you for everything, Detective."

The detective glances back at Jace. I sense that he might be figuring out the same thing I did earlier. My stomach drops to my feet. I open my mouth to say something, and then I let it go.

"I'll be in touch, Mrs. Miller," he says.

Jace holds my hand on the way back to the house. I shed my coat and shoes. I stumble into the kitchen, and then I collapse onto a chair, completely exhausted. Jace follows me, but he hovers in the doorway.

I don't look at him as I say, "Tell me why you did it."

"Wh-what?"

Then I turn to him. "Tell me why you doctored that photo and put it online."

His face pales.

"I'm not stupid. I know you can do things like that, or at least know someone who can. You've been off with me for weeks. You keep calling me a liar, and I know you're mad at me for something."

Jace doubles over. He's sobbing now, and the sound is awful, like a hurt animal.

"Why?" The word slides from my tongue like grease. My mouth is oily. Maybe I'm getting ready to vomit.

My own son did this to me. He sabotaged me. He threw me to the Internet wolves and watched them tear me to shreds. He watched my business crumble, everything I'd worked for. All this time and all this anguish came from my son's anger. I don't understand it.

"Because!" Jace roars, pain contorting his expression, cheeks flaming, burning, smoldering red. "I know you cheated on Dad!"

The garage door leading into the house swings open, and standing there at the threshold is Rick.

Chapter 27
HOLLY

I'm doing the right thing. I know I am. It will all work out in the end. I just have to keep telling myself that.

Even so, I'm a nervous wreck. My palms are clammy, and my heart is thundering around in my chest like my body is caught in a violent storm.

I squeeze my hands into fists, shut my eyes tight, and count to five, drawing in a deep breath. I won't freak out now. I won't break down. I have come so far. Just a little closer, then everything will be okay. It'll all be out in the open. I did what I had to do to keep us safe.

I did this to make everything right again.

The room is small, suffocating, but I can cope with it here. There's a tiny kitchen with a hot plate, microwave, and sink. The single bed is fine just for me, and I can put Lissa in the tiny cot next to it. Right now she's still in her stroller, napping. I start to pace back and forth, feet padding on the dark-red carpet. My eyes linger on the threadbare sections. I spot a cockroach and almost scream.

"Everything is going to be okay," I say to myself.

Maybe if I keep saying it, I'll believe it.

Finally, my phone screen lights up through the darkness. I look at it, and it nearly slips through my sweaty grasp.

A text message. I read it once then again.

What does he know?

I wait a beat, thinking. I type a reply.

Everything. And he's going to hurt me. I need to lie low now.

What's my next move? I just don't know. It's dark and cold in this sweat-scented motel. I'm afraid, not only of the consequences of my actions but of what will happen now—right now in this moment. Where I'll go. How I'll get out of this alive.

The screen lights up again.

What does Audrey know?

I respond: *I don't know. I've been lying to her.*

Beside me, Lissa cries in her stroller. I try to soothe her by pushing it back and forth. It's not enough. She's tired, cold, and hungry too.

She continues to fuss, rubbing at her eyes with her little dimpled fists. Her cheeks are red, and I feel so guilty that she's ended up caught in this web.

But I had no choice.

I search through my backpack and lean against the wall, sighing. I mutter a defeated "shit." I don't have a bottle.

I'm in over my head. I didn't think this through. I had to get out of there fast. But now I'm stuck here unprepared,

The Nanny's Secret

frightened, and alone with a six-month-old baby and no supplies.

Another text message brings light to the darkness.

I think you need to tell Audrey now. She could get hurt too. He could be with her.

I stand up and lift Lissa from her stroller, walking in circles with her, bouncing her, hoping she'll calm down and fall asleep. But she's hungry, and the only way to fix that is to give her something to eat.

Maybe it's time to bring it all out in the open. There are more people at risk than just me.

Chapter 28

Rick's eyes widen. "What the hell is going on?"

I turn slowly on my heel in his direction. Every part of my body feels limp and bloodless. I don't know how much he heard or how long he's been standing there.

"Holly has kidnapped Lissa." The words are so quiet that I'm not sure he even heard me.

Rick's dumbfounded expression twists so suddenly, it's like I've just slapped him across the face.

He lifts his fingers to his temples and shakes his head, blinking in disbelief. "Wait a minute. How... How do you know Holly took Lissa?"

"She isn't here, and neither is Lissa. She isn't answering her phone, and she sent Jace a really weird text message to say sorry." I wrap my arms around my body when I realize I'm shivering. "I've reported Lissa as missing. The only lead the police have is that Elijah saw Holly pushing the stroller—"

The Nanny's Secret

"Why would Holly take her? This doesn't make sense." He clutches hold of the wall as though keeping himself upright.

"It's after dark, Rick. If this was all a misunderstanding, she'd let me, or you, or Jace know where she is. She has our *baby*, Rick."

His eyes flash with anger. "Fuck!" And then he catches himself. I see his eyes trail over to our son, who's still hovering in the doorway. "Jace. You okay, buddy?"

Rick walks over to him and wraps an arm around his shoulder. Full of adrenaline, I step past them both and make my way into the living room. I need to see the neighborhood. If Holly is going to return with my baby, I need to be the first one to see her. I begin to fantasize about it. My imagination conjures their shapes walking down the drive. Holly has Lissa on her hip. She's wearing that same Alice band. Her shoes are a polished black. Lissa's blond hair shines under the streetlight. She's smiling. Her blue-gray eyes look up to the nanny. I squeeze my eyes shut.

When I open them, Elijah is rushing over to the house.

I hurry to the front door and start down the sidewalk. According to Stalks, Elijah was the last person to see Holly. I may hate the guy, but I need answers from him.

"Is everything okay over here? I thought I heard a shout," Elijah says, stopping on the sidewalk when he reaches me. He stands beneath the streetlamp, bathed in its light.

It hits me then, everything that's happened. My head is fuzzy as though the world is spinning. "My baby is missing." The words choke out of me, and I just manage to hold back a sob.

Elijah straightens. The breeze grazes his dark-blond hair. His blue eyes are razor sharp. They cut a deep slice through my heart. "Don't you mean *our* baby?" Each word is like a sledgehammer to my chest.

I wring my hands. I can't draw in enough air. Elijah takes a step toward me, leaving no more than an inch between us. He stares down at me, a sly smile spreading across his face.

"I want you to say it. Admit it out loud. Lissa is *my* baby, *my* flesh and blood. *Our* baby. Because *I'm* the real father. *I'm* the one who got you pregnant, not Rick."

His words shiver down my spine. I swallow hard as the trees and the mailboxes and the other houses spin around me.

"Say it," Elijah barks out. "Say I'm the father. Lissa looks just like me. There's no denying it anymore, Audrey. You can't hide behind that perfect wife, perfect suburban façade anymore. You're not as high and mighty as you think. There's nothing pure about you."

"All right!" I scream, if for no other reason than to make him stop talking, make him stop firing round after round of these hateful words at me like dozens of shotgun bullets hitting me all at once. "She's your baby. Is that what you want to hear? Are you happy to ruin my life, kick me when I'm down?"

Rick's footsteps pound the pavement behind me. "What the hell is going on?"

Elijah's shrewd eyes whirl to Rick then back to me.

The Nanny's Secret

"Why don't you tell him, Audrey? Tell Rick the dirty little secret you've been hiding from him. Because if you're right about Lissa, we all need to know the truth, don't we?" That slimy, sociopathic voice. I can't stand it.

Rick's eyes flick over to Elijah and then land on me. Dark eyes. Like Jace's but nothing like Lissa's light-gray eyes. Deep down, I've always known it would be impossible to pretend. I've been living a lie, and like most lies, when they surface, they create a chasm between the liar and their family.

"I... Lissa... She's not... Elijah and I... It was only one night, I swear... but I got pregnant. The baby... is not yours, Rick. I h-hate him so much, and I h-hate myself for what I did... but it's done now... and I can't take it back." I trip over every word, crying so hard I can barely catch my breath. Tears stream down my face, blurring my vision to where Rick is only a watery blob in front of me.

"I think what she's trying to say is that Lissa is *my* baby." Elijah smirks.

Then I hear Rick groan. The sound is primal. I watch him plow past me. He arcs his arm back and slams his fist down hard onto Elijah. His fist crashes into the side of Elijah's jaw. Elijah wails, more in shock and surprise than in pain, reeling back. Rick takes advantage while Elijah is stumbling back on his feet to land another crushing blow to Elijah's eye.

I hear something crack. I don't know whether it's Rick's knuckles or Elijah's cheek, eye socket, jaw, whatever. I don't want to know. I'm rooted in place, my brain screaming at me to push myself between them to make them stop.

Jace appears in the doorway. "Mom, do something!"

Elijah pitches forward, knocking Rick back. Soon they're a tumble of limbs, both landing blows. I pull myself out of the shock that has kept me still, and I'm about to reach for my phone to call the police when a patrol car rolls up. It must be the officer Detective Stalks promised.

"Go inside, Jace," I call out.

Jace is frozen like a block of ice.

"Do it!" The warning sting in my voice whips him back to reality, and he races back inside.

"I'm going to kill you!" Rick yells. "You slept with my wife? You will never see that baby again, whether she's yours or not."

Bruises, cuts, and scrapes are all over their exposed skin. The collar of Rick's shirt is torn, dangling off his arm. I try to put myself between them, but Elijah's elbow collides with my stomach. It knocks the breath from my lungs. My knees slam into the ground. Fingers splayed in the grass, I gasp for oxygen.

Rick and Elijah break apart, chests heaving, and the officers take guarded steps toward them. A moment later, both men are in cuffs, and I stand there, dumbfounded by it all.

While one of the officers works up paperwork for Rick and Elijah, the other walks up to me.

He has a round belly. Freckles pepper his nose and cheekbones. His lips are wet and red underneath a thick and bushy ginger-colored beard.

The Nanny's Secret

"Quite the evening you're having here, Mrs..."

"Miller," I say.

"Nice to meet you. I'm Officer Stevens. Can you fill me in on everything going on?"

I nod and pull in a deep breath. If I ever want to see my baby again, I have to tell the truth, all of it. Lissa's life depends on it.

Chapter 29

"I'm going to jot down some notes here on my pad." Officer Stevens taps a pen against a mini notebook. "But the bodycam I'm wearing will record everything we're saying, providing both audio and video footage. Are you okay with all this?"

"Yes." I wring my hands. "Let's get on with it, please. Every second counts."

I answer everything I can, as truthfully as I can. I confess to sleeping with Elijah. When Officer Stevens calls it an affair, I clarify that it was a one-night stand but confirm that the likelihood of Elijah being Lissa's father is high.

"She looks like him," I say, finally uttering the words I've been holding on to for a very long time. "My husband and I have had trouble conceiving a child since Jace was born twelve years ago. I... I lost a baby about four months before I slept with..." My shaking hand travels to my mouth. I don't like thinking about that night. It blurs

The Nanny's Secret

around the edges. The drinks, the weight of him on top of me, the awareness that this man was not my husband. I close my eyes and slowly open them again. "Rick and I never got checked out because we were happy as a one-child family. But I stayed off contraception just in case." Officer Stevens hands me a tissue. "Sorry, this probably isn't relevant. But it just seems clear to me that Lissa is Elijah's daughter, even though I really don't want her to be."

"All right," the officer says. "That's enough about the fight and the affair. Let's concentrate on getting your baby back. Detective Stalks has filled me in on all the events. It sounds like you've been the target of some online harassment."

"Yes," I say. "But that wasn't Holly."

"How do you know that?" he asks.

I try not to look at Jace. "The person who did it confessed to me, and it's personal, so I don't want to talk about it. They have nothing to do with Lissa's disappearance. But I don't know who slashed my tires earlier. That could be connected."

Stevens's eyes narrow. "Are you sure you don't want to tell me?"

I nod.

"All right. Well, I'm going to take a look at the nanny's bedroom, if that's all right."

"Go ahead," I say.

I glance over at my son, hovering in the living room doorway, taking in his bloodshot eyes and tear-streaked face. No matter that he's almost a teenager. He's still just a kid. A stupid kid who wanted to get back at his mom for making an awful mistake. I'm not mad at him, just mad at myself. I walk over to him and place an arm over his shoulder.

"Is Dad going to be okay?" Jace asks.

"He'll be just fine. He's at the police station right now. He's in a little trouble at the moment because of the fight, but it's nothing we can't deal with." I don't tell him that Rick could potentially lose his job if he's convicted of a crime.

"What about Lissa and Holly?" he asks.

My heart twists. I need to believe that Holly is at least taking care of Lissa. But I don't understand why Holly has taken my child. All this time I suspected Holly of either targeting me or going after my husband, but I never thought for one moment that she might steal my child. The thought makes me nauseous, but I still try to smile and tell Jace everything is going to be okay.

We follow Stevens upstairs as he searches Holly's room. It's hauntingly quiet in there. Holly hasn't done much to personalize the room. There are no family photographs. Her clothes are neatly put away in the closet. Jace and I stand in the hallway, peeking in through the doorframe. The room smells bad, which is odd considering how neat it is. But there's a definite sewer smell drifting out into the corridor.

Officer Stevens looks up at me from his crouched position on the carpet. "Ma'am, is there any reason why the nanny would have dirty diapers underneath her bed?"

The Nanny's Secret

"Dirty... diapers? She was keeping dirty diapers under her bed?" I step into the room to get a better view.

"Looks that way." He slips a diaper into an evidence bag and seals it.

I stare at him in shock.

"Do you have any idea why she may have done that?" Stevens asks.

I frown. "None whatsoever." She always seemed clean and organized. This revelation is way out of left field from her usual behavior.

Stevens reaches back under the bed with a gloved hand. I watch, feeling impotent, as he pulls out another bulky item.

"A used baby bottle," he says. "It's a bit odd to be hoarding dirty items like this." His eyes roam across the room. "She doesn't seem like the type."

I stare at the bottle. It has a residue of formula at the bottom, but it's been drained, most likely by Lissa. The bottle gets bagged too.

An unsettled sensation creeps across my spine. Is Holly obsessed with Lissa? Does she wish she was Lissa's mother, and that's why she took her? I'm still missing several pieces, still have so many unanswered questions, but at least the police are involved now. At least I know I'm not paranoid.

"Is this her laptop?" Officer Stevens asks, lifting it from under the mattress of Holly's bed, where she apparently slid it to hide it.

"I don't recognize it." I glance at Jace. "Do you?"

He rubs his elbow with his hand. "It's... I think it's Elijah's."

"Elijah's?" I turn to my son, surprised. "Are you sure?"

Jace shrugs, uncertainty shadowing his face. "I think so. I've seen it in his home office before." He points to the left corner of the laptop cover. "I remember the scratch. It was on his desk."

Until recently, Jace was close with Elijah's older children and would often go to their house to hang out or play. He would certainly have a better idea of what belongs over there than I do. And as I have the thought, I realize I now know the reason Jace doesn't like to be around Elijah's children anymore. It's because of me and Elijah. The shame makes my skin burn.

"We'll take it to the lab to have our technicians perform a forensic sweep of the hard drive," Officer Stevens says. "I'll just need your written consent."

"Uh, yes. Sure. Of course." I'm still in such disbelief at what they're finding in this room that I stumble over the words.

The officer takes the evidence back downstairs, but I remain where I am with Jace. I want a quick word with him on his own.

"Jace, have you ever noticed Holly acting suspiciously with Lissa? Anything odd or—not even odd—just something that stood out? It could really help. Think carefully," I say, watching his face screw up with concentration.

This whole time I've been distracted by the viral photo and my guilt about what happened with Elijah. I wonder what signs I've missed.

Jace scratches the back of his neck. "She...She knew that you had... that you, um... the thing with Elijah." His eyes flicker downward. He can't even say it.

"How?" I ask.

"I... I told her." He stares down at his feet, and I think he might cry again, but he doesn't.

And then I think I might cry, too, but I somehow hold it together. "Jace, how did you know about me and Elijah?"

"I saw you," he says. "It was... You were on the sofa, and I was in bed. I came downstairs to get a glass of water, and he was on top of you."

My knees buckle. I grab hold of the wall for support.

"And... and I kinda lied when I said I saw the laptop on Elijah's desk. I mean, it wasn't a lie. It just wasn't the whole truth. It was near you. On the coffee table."

Elijah had brought the laptop with him when he came to check in on me that night. Rick was away for work, and I was still grieving the miscarriage. I'd had a conversation with Elijah in his garden. One of those quick chats that suddenly grows deeper, and you're not sure how. We'd announced that I was pregnant to Emma and Elijah a week before the miscarriage. Rick blindsided me with the announcement at a cookout. Then, of course, Elijah had asked about the pregnancy. I told him about our loss, and somehow, I also confessed my concern that I would never get pregnant again.

When Rick was out of town, Elijah hurried over to the house to show me something on his laptop. He'd seemed breathless. Like he was excited to show me. It was nothing, really. An article about rainbow babies—children conceived after the mother has suffered a miscarriage—with some accounts from mothers about how happy they were. Well, I was an emotional mess, and it just happened to be what I needed. Elijah suggested we open some wine and I talk to him about what I was feeling.

Everything after that moment makes me feel sick when I think about it.

I turn to Jace. "Did Holly ever tell you she thought Lissa might be Elijah's baby?"

Jace stares at the floor and nods. "She knew."

"She knew... what?"

"That Lissa is Elijah's kid." He mumbles the words, his cheeks turning red.

Another puzzle piece slots into place. I think I know why Holly kept the diapers, kept the bottles. She was trying to gain DNA evidence. But why did she steal Elijah's laptop? Why risk everything by breaking into his house like that? Why storm into our lives and destroy two families, especially when there are innocent people at risk of getting hurt? What's in it for her?

I need that last piece, and if I don't figure out what it is, I might never see my daughter ever again.

Chapter 30

Rick makes bail a few hours later and arrives home in the dark, sporting a busted lip and a black eye. I'm sitting on the sofa with Jace asleep with his head on my lap. I have my mobile phone out next to me, waiting to hear from the police. Officer Stevens has left for the night, and Detective Stalks checked in over the phone but hasn't been back to the house.

"Lissa?" he asks.

I shake my head, starting to cry.

There's so much pain in the look Rick and I exchange. Not just because Lissa is missing but everything else. I want to find the words that will make it all better, but there's nothing I can do or say.

"I don't... I don't even want to look at you right now, Audrey," he says between gritted teeth. "But for the sake of that little girl... The girl I thought..." His voice cracks, and he turns away. "I need to know what the police are doing to find her."

"They've been around the neighborhood, looking for witnesses, and they're searching the area."

He sets his keys down on the table, followed by his wallet. "It's not enough." He sits down in a chair opposite me, and his shoulders slump. I've never seen my husband look so defeated. "I should go out there."

"It's dark," I say. "There's not much you can do. They have an AMBER Alert going too."

"Okay," he says softly.

I stroke Jace's hair as she sleeps soundly. "I made a mistake, Rick. I'm so sorry."

"You've ruined our lives, Audrey." His chin wobbles. "As soon as Lissa is found, I'm filing for divorce."

The sob catches in my throat. All I can do is nod. "Okay. If that's what you want."

Silently, he rises from the chair and makes his way upstairs to bed. I watch his back disappear into the shadows.

Jace rolls away and makes himself comfortable on the other side of the sofa, so I rise and wander onto the porch, needing some fresh air. All I can think about is the pain etched across Rick's face. We've had our problems in the past, but I've never seen him like that. So utterly disgusted with me.

It's what I deserve. Deep down, I always knew this day would come. I had hoped that I would be able to gently convince Rick to move to another neighborhood, but he loves it so much here.

I turn to leave when a man's face pops out from around the side of the house. I gasp and nearly jump out of my

The Nanny's Secret

skin, heart bashing against my ribcage. And then I realize it's Elijah, and my blood runs hot with anger.

"You have to stop showing up like this on my property." I cut him a scathing glare.

His expression is sincere when he says, "I'm sorry. For all of this." The streetlight highlights stitches above his eyebrow and a bruise along his cheekbone.

I sit on the bottom porch step and place my head in my hands, resting my elbows on my knees. "You should go. You'll only make things worse. Rick can barely look at me, so if he sees me talking to you... He wants a divorce. My baby is missing, and my husband wants a divorce."

"That's tough. I'm sorry." He sounds like he means it, but I don't look at him. I hide behind my hands because it seems like the best option for me right now.

Neither of us speak for several moments. I'm tired in my bones. I'm too drained to argue with Elijah right now.

"Have you heard anything about Lissa?" Elijah asks in a soft, concerned voice.

I finally glance up. "Not yet."

"What are you going to do?"

"There's an AMBER Alert out. The police are working on it. I'm thinking about places where I can look for them. But I don't know where Holly might have taken her."

"Do you think Holly is unhinged?"

I scowl at him. "Of course I think she's unhinged. She stole my baby."

"I know, but do you think she'd actually... *hurt* Lissa?" Elijah's eyes flash with something. Concern. Worry. I don't know how much of it is for him and his situation or how much is reserved for Lissa, if any at all.

I study him for a moment, debating what to tell him, what to leave out. "I don't think so."

"Do you have any idea where she could've gone?"

"No. But the police searched her bedroom and found some... peculiar things."

Elijah sits down next to me, but I inch away from him. "You probably shouldn't sit so close to me."

Elijah licks his lips and stands, brushing his hands together. "Sorry. You're probably right. What did the police find in Holly's room?"

"Used diapers." I cringe, thinking about the smell and mess again.

Elijah's nose crinkles with disgust. His skin pales to the same shade as the moon hanging low in the sky. I debate whether to tell him about the laptop, about my suspicion that she's trying to gather DNA evidence that he's Lissa's father and not Rick. Something in my gut tells me not to trust Elijah, to not give him that ammunition of information.

My phone vibrates in my back pocket. I pluck it out and tap the screen to wake it. There's a message from a number I don't recognize. Elijah studies me, his expression guarded.

"What is it?"

My first instinct is to lie. I don't know how much involvement I want from Elijah right now. I need to be careful what I say to him.

"It's just one of the officers wanting to confirm a few

things." I stand up, my legs weak, my pulse thundering through my eardrums. "I have to go. I'll let you know if I hear anything about Lissa."

His eyes narrow as I return to the house. I close the door behind me and look out the window, watching him until he crosses the street and returns to his house. I wait until I see him walk inside and close the door.

Then, with my pulse quaking through my veins, I look at the text message again.

Meet me at the motel on Sycamore Road. Room 45. Come alone or this won't work. Do not tell anyone, or I won't come out. I swear it. Please bring baby formula and a bottle. - Holly.

A queasy sensation gnaws at my stomach. It's quiet in the house. Rick must still be upstairs. Jace is sleeping. Now is my chance. On a whim, I go with my impulse. I jog to the kitchen, swipe Rick's car keys from the table where he left them. After grabbing a can of formula and a bottle of water to mix it, I head to the garage.

My heart is a wild, bucking bronco in my chest as I get into Rick's car. I crank the ignition and steer down the driveway, pulling out carefully. At the entrance of the neighborhood, I glance in my rearview mirror. Relieved that Elijah isn't following me, I tap the address Holly gave me into my GPS—its's about a fifteen-minute drive—and pull out of my neighborhood, praying all the while that I'm not going to be walking straight into a trap.

Chapter 31

The GPS navigation takes me to a seedy two-story motel on the outskirts of town. A sign in the front reads "Vacancy. Hot water. Cabl TV." The e at the end of the word cable is missing.

I shut the engine off. My hands are shaking. I should be running out of this car and breaking down the door, but now that I'm here, the dread is pinning me to this spot. Then Holly's face appears between two grimy drapes. It sparks a fire in me. I'm out of the car, rushing toward Holly's room. She has the door open before I reach it.

"Come in," she says in a hurried voice.

"Lissa?" I ask, rushing into the room.

The air is stale, and there's a faint hint of cigarette smell. Holly lifts a bawling Lissa from her car seat. My poor baby is red in the face, her eyes swollen and glossy.

"How long has she been crying like this?" I ask.

"Almost since we got here. Did you bring the formula?"

The Nanny's Secret

"Yes." I hand it to Holly while she gives me the baby.

She shovels out three scoops and puts it in the bottle and shakes it to incorporate the powder with the water.

"There's no microwave, so this will have to do," she says.

She tries to reach for Lissa once the bottle is prepared, but I flinch and take a step away from her. "Give me the bottle. There's no way I'm handing my baby to you ever again."

Holly nods, passing me the bottle. Then she sighs. "I'm sorry. For everything. This is all just a huge mess. I didn't mean for it to get out of control like this."

I sit down on a faded chair and feed my baby while Holly half flops down onto the bed.

"You kidnapped my baby," I remind her.

Holly's eyes drift to mine, shimmering with tears. "Have you told the police where I am?"

I don't answer her. Everything happened so fast that I rushed out here without calling Detective Stalks.

"I didn't mean for any of this to happen," Holly says. "I just... I freaked out." She pauses a beat and then mumbles, "I didn't technically kidnap her."

"You left without telling me where you were going, while you were under my employ and while you were caring for my child. You wouldn't answer your phone. What exactly would you call it then, if not kidnapping?"

A muscle in Holly's jaw twitches.

"Holly, I'm going to tell you what I'm going to do now. I'm taking my baby home. Are you going to try to stop me?"

She shakes her head.

"Good. But before I go, I have one question. Are you going to tell me what's going on?" I can't stop thinking about the dirty diapers and Elijah's laptop in her room. "Because I know it's connected to Elijah. And I think it's something I need to know before I take Lissa back to a house opposite his house."

"Yes," she says. "But you're not going to like what I have to say."

I gaze down at my daughter in my arms. She's warm. She smells like milk and lavender and the detergent I use at home. She's mine. Not Elijah's. Maybe not even Rick's, as much as I hate to say it. I wish it was otherwise, but it isn't. Lissa is my rainbow baby, and I know in this moment that I will do anything for her. I would die for her. Kill for her.

"Just tell me," I say to Holly.

"All right." She pulls in a deep breath. "I grew up with a single mother." She rubs her palms against her thighs and stretches out her legs. She looks uncomfortable, but she continues. "My mom was great. It was hard, but she did her best, and she always loved me. My childhood was decent, nice even. I always had something to eat and a warm bed to sleep in. But... there was something missing. I've always had a deep-rooted need to find out who my father is. My mother never told me. I didn't press her, but I had a feeling she didn't want me to know. I had a feeling that something bad happened between them."

"Go on," I say.

"I... I ordered a DNA kit," she says. "One of those online tests. And when I got the results, I found out who

The Nanny's Secret

my father is." She shakes her head slightly. "I guess he did the online test too. Maybe he wanted to see if he had other children out there."

"Elijah," I say.

Holly sighs. "Yes. Elijah Johnson is my father."

Chapter 32
ELIJAH - YESTERDAY

He has a sense of it all unraveling, like all his secrets are about to be pulled from a thread spool. There's no more time for drinking and moping, only for ensuring life can go on as he wants it. Because what is his life worth if he can't do what he wants?

Elijah has always known deep down that he's special. His mother made him feel special. She told him he would grow up to be an amazing father and man. *You could be an astronaut if you want to be. But there's nothing better in this world than being a parent. There's no better purpose for a man than becoming a father.*

Well, he sure fulfilled that wish.

His own father was nothing like his mother. Bill Johnson didn't care for children too much, though he did like to act like the top dog whenever he was in public. Part of that was showing off his son to the neighbors. Bill Johnson was certainly a proud man.

The Nanny's Secret

Elijah carried that on in his own way.

The house is quiet now that all the kids are with Emma's parents, so he slips out onto the driveway. He hasn't had a drink all morning, though he wonders if there's still some bourbon in his system. If there is, so be it. He's talked his way out of parking tickets before. Who knows? Maybe he could do it for a DUI too.

The nanny from across the street is at home with his daughter Lissa. He's always known Lissa is his. When Rick and Audrey moved into the neighborhood, Elijah took one look at Audrey and knew he wanted her. That body—and a nice face too—but it was the way she looked at her husband and son that made him want her. He knew he had to bide his time, though. Audrey wasn't the kind of woman to stray easily.

He'd watched and waited over the years until he noticed a pattern. Rick worked too hard, leaving her alone for a significant amount of time. And then Elijah found out that Audrey had lost a baby.

Audrey was ripe for the picking.

It took just once to make Lissa. Not bad going.

Elijah continues to his car, casting one quick glance at the house. He doesn't want Audrey coming home too early, so he drives up to her floral shop and parks up the street. He's dressed all in black and has on a ski mask to hide his identity from the security cameras at the back of the shop. He saw Audrey unloading them from her car recently. Considering someone has been harassing her, it's no surprise.

Hopefully Audrey will assume what he's about to do is related to the harassment and not even suspect him.

Angling himself to the left of the camera so that he's on the periphery, not in the center, he manages to hit the camera with a rock before he hurries over to her car to slash the tires. Two should do it. Most people only carry one spare tire.

He doesn't need to worry about Rick. The guy is never home. He parks on his drive and then heads around the back of Audrey and Rick's house, listening carefully. It's a sunny day, and he remembers how the nanny said she liked to take Lissa out in the yard during good weather.

Sure enough, he hears the telltale giggle of his daughter followed by Holly's voice as she offers Lissa a sun hat. He needs to know what the hell that nanny's deal is. So he hops the fence, much to the surprise of the young woman. She immediately goes to the baby to pick her up off the picnic blanket, but Elijah is faster. He closes the distance between them with just a few strides and clutches Holly's elbow.

"What the hell are you doing?" Holly tries to pull back, but Elijah keeps a firm grip on her.

"I could ask you the same thing, young lady," he says. She squirms but can't wrench herself free. "Who the fuck are you, and what are you doing in this neighborhood? Because I know you're up to something. I've seen you watching my house from your bedroom window. I have a pretty good suspicion that you broke into my property too."

"I don't know what you're talking about!" she says.

"Cut the act. There was a pretty dainty-looking shoe

print under our kitchen window. And I doubt it was Audrey's."

When her face pales, he can't help but grin. So he was right. She had broken in and taken the laptop. He stares at the girl, at her blue eyes and light-brown hair. There's something about her that seems so familiar to him. The girl is hot, in a way. She has a nice figure. A firm ass, perky tits. She hides it, though, most of the time.

"Get off me," Holly says, spitting the words from between her teeth.

"No." He glances at his daughter Lissa. "Tell me why you're here or I'll hurt her."

"You're insane!" Her eyes widen. She's rattled. He can feel it.

"I'm just a man protecting my family," he says.

She scoffs at that, and then she starts to laugh. He's confused. He almost lets her go.

"What the hell are you laughing at?" he demands.

"A man protecting his family." Her grin is mocking. It twists easily into a grimace. "What about the family right in front of your face? What about us?"

He frowns. She knows about Lissa? She knows about him and Audrey?

"You're so stupid," Holly says. "You've had so many kids, you don't even recognize your own. Well, here I am. I'm your daughter."

The fog clears from his mind. Of course she's his. That's why she looks so familiar. Though he will retract those thoughts about her tits and ass. But what the hell is she doing here, nannying for the neighbors?

"So what?" he says. "I've got a few kids with women who wanted nothing to do with me. It's not my fault if they wanted to raise the baby alone. What? Are you looking for a handout?"

"God, you're disgusting," she says. "No. I'm here for payback."

Chapter 33

The motel walls feel like they're closing in. Gently, I ease the bottle from Lissa's mouth and move her onto my shoulder, rubbing her back. Despite everything that has happened with Holly, she still grabs a muslin cloth, and with a little nod from me to allow her to do it, she places it on my shoulder to catch any spit-up.

"So you came to work across the street from your father," I say.

Holly wraps her arms across her chest. "Yes."

"Why?"

She sits back down on the bed. "It's... It makes sense when I explain it." She sighs. "I didn't just match with Elijah's DNA. I found some brothers and sisters too." She bites her lip slightly. "He has a lot of kids."

"Other than...?"

"Yes," she says. "Like *lots* more. From my age, all the way down to just born. And I've been in contact with them because... because of what he does."

Despite Lissa's warmth, my blood feels freezing cold.

"He's obsessed with getting women pregnant," Holly continues. "He gets off on it."

My throat is dry, and my voice cracks when I try to speak. "How many?"

"I know of thirteen other children. Thirteen brothers and sisters," she says. "Including my half sister Lissa." She pulls in a deep breath. "I'm the oldest, I think, and for that reason I felt like I had a responsibility to stop this from happening again. Especially considering what he does to our mothers."

"What does he do?" My voice sounds weak and thin. An echo in a tin can.

"Sit down, Audrey." Holly gestures to a chair. "Maybe put Lissa in her stroller for a moment."

"No," I whisper.

"Please," she says. "I know I've broken your trust, but you need to do this. I don't want you to collapse and hurt Lissa."

So much tension is balled up in my body that I do as she says. But I pull the stroller over to the chair and place it right next to me when I sit.

Holly wipes away a tear. "I'm sorry to have to tell you this. Please know that I like you a lot, Audrey. You probably hate me, but I like you and always have. Apologize to Jace for me. I manipulated him to get to the truth, but it was only because I want this all to end."

"Just spit it out, Holly."

"I'd seen a picture of Elijah online before I took this job. As soon as I saw Lissa's blond hair and gray eyes, I

The Nanny's Secret

suspected her of being Elijah's daughter. I also suspected that Jace knew, considering how resentful and rude he was to you. So I asked him to tell me a secret. He told me he saw you and Elijah having sex on the sofa. Only what he described did not sound like sex. It sounded like rape."

I grip the chair, afraid I might slip out of it. "No, I... I let him into the house. I was drunk, but—"

"Audrey, Jace saw your eyes closed and your body hanging half off the sofa." She inches forward as though she wants to come over and comfort me. "And Elijah's done this before." Her voice softens. "I'm in contact with my brothers and sisters. We've shared stories. We know he does this, and his victims—our mothers—are too ashamed to go to the police because they're always in a relationship with someone else."

My stomach lurches when she says the word "victim." I was a pawn in Elijah's twisted little game. I think of the way he used to top up my wine and separate me from the group during neighborhood gatherings. How he'd make little comments about Rick never being there for me. He comforted me when I was upset about not being able to get pregnant. He was there, waiting, after my second miscarriage when Rick was away at a conference. He groomed me meticulously, so slow and deep, unassumingly.

But then he still had to go that one step further.

Hot tears sting my eyes, blur my vision.

"He has pills that he puts in his victims' drinks," Audrey says. "My half brother Sam overheard his mother telling her sister about it. Sam and I have been texting this whole time because he wanted me to get Elijah's laptop."

I try to pull my focus back to Holly, but the room is spinning. Elijah *raped* me. He's not just a cad or a womanizer, he's a rapist who likes to father children. Who *needs* to father children and spread his seed.

"I can't imagine what else he does in order to get women pregnant," Holly says. "Pokes holes in condoms, lies about wearing one. He's disgusting—"

"What did you say about a laptop?" I ask. "Why would you take it?"

"Sam said his mother suspected that Elijah recorded the rape. That she came in and out of unconsciousness and seemed to remember a camera there. And this cropped up in a few stories. I thought if I got the laptop, I might be able to find the videos. But they weren't there. He must store them somewhere else."

"Jace said he saw the laptop on the coffee table when he walked in on us." I press my hand to my mouth, holding in the urge to vomit. Once I'm composed, I say, "If it was open, he might have recorded me too."

She nods. "The files aren't stored on the laptop, though. He might have used it to record you, but he probably downloaded it onto a USB stick and wiped it from the hard drive."

"It makes sense," I say. "He wouldn't want Emma finding it."

I wipe my forehead, and my hand comes away soaked in sweat. "This is all so horrible."

"I know," she says. "I'm sorry."

"The police searched your room. They found dirty

diapers under your bed and dirty bottles in the back of your closet."

Holly nods. "I wanted to run a paternity test. But I couldn't do it because she's a minor, and you need permission. I needed Elijah's ID too. I was running into dead ends."

"Why?"

"I thought that if I couldn't get the video evidence of him raping women, I could at least provide Emma with evidence that her husband fathered a child next door." She shakes her head. "I thought if I brought all that out into the open, Emma would pay attention. I think I was born before they got married, so me being his daughter wouldn't be enough to break them up. Most of my half brothers and sisters didn't want to be involved. This is all very hard for them. So I thought if I could prove that Lissa is his daughter, I could at least get Emma away from him."

"I can't believe this," I whisper. Next to me, Lissa is sleeping. Her delicate straw-colored eyelashes rest against pink cheeks.

"Well, it's all true. Elijah either tricks women into carrying his child, or he rapes them. My mother was so young and impressionable when she met him, she fell into his trap. She believed he was a good man, and it was too late before she knew the truth." Holly's light eyes go blackout dark. "He'll sleep with any woman with a pulse to get what he wants. He'll mess with their birth control, tell them what they want to hear to charm them into bed. He'll drug them and record them. Next thing they know, their whole world is rocked when they find out they're pregnant. They deal with the consequences. They raise the children, and Elijah gets to continue his sick little fetish with the next woman." Holly stares at me, unblinking, eyes swimming with tears, lips twisted into a grimace. "He has to be stopped."

"Holly," I say. "I understand why you applied for the job in my home, and I understand why you broke into Elijah's home and stole his laptop. But what I don't understand is why you took my daughter."

"Because he threatened me," she says. "And I got scared. He told me he'd hurt Lissa, and I panicked." A sob escapes from her chest, and instinctually, I get up, cross the room, and wrap my arms around her.

Chapter 34

"Tell me everything," I say.

She sniffs, bringing her sobs under control. "I was in the backyard with Lissa. We were playing on a blanket. It was a nice day, sunny afternoon. No one was home. It was just Lissa and me. Elijah jumped over the fence. I ended up telling him who I really am, and he got angry." She brushes tears away as she composes herself to speak. "I blurted everything out and made it all worse. I told him I was looking into getting proof that he fathered all these children, and I was going to lay it all out to Emma. That's when he lunged at me, telling me that he would never let me do that."

"Oh, Holly."

"The next thing I knew, his hands were wrapped around my throat. I couldn't breathe. His fingers pressed into my windpipe. I started getting dizzy. I heard Lissa crying on the blanket on the grass. I knew I had to get away, for her, for myself. I kicked him in the groin. It was enough that he let go of me and stumbled backward. I grabbed Lissa. He lunged at me again and called me a bitch. I didn't... I didn't think. I was just on the move. I found the stroller by the back gate and put Lissa in it. We ran away, through people's yards, across lawns. Elijah didn't chase us far. I don't think he wanted anyone to see him following us because it was broad daylight. I didn't really look behind me until we got a few blocks away, at the end of the neighborhood. That's when I looked back and realized we'd lost him."

"I'm so sorry," I say. I think about my slashed tires timing up with Elijah's confrontation with Holly. It can't be coincidental. Then he gave incorrect information to the police to slow things down even further. Even him coming over like that, fighting with Rick, could all have been a way to distract us from finding Holly and Lissa.

He must be searching for Holly too. He's dangerous now. A man trying to hide his secrets.

Holly's damp lashes blink in my direction. "I didn't want to take Lissa, but I had no choice. We were running for our lives. My phone died. I went and got a burner from the gas station to be able to call you. Plus, I didn't want to risk Elijah seeing my number on your phone if he happened to be with you at the time I called you."

"That explains the number I didn't recognize."

"I'm glad you answered. I never meant to scare you or get the police involved. I just didn't know what else to do. I knew I'd taken your baby and what you'd think. I thought if I got arrested, then no one would believe me about Elijah, and he'd win all over again."

The Nanny's Secret

Holly cradles her head in her hands. Her shoulders shake with heavy sobs.

I can understand it now. I see a young girl panicking under pressure. I see her life flashing before her eyes. Not just from Elijah's attack but also the opportunity to make Elijah pay for his crimes.

I rub her back. "It's going to be all right. We're going to figure this out."

Holly stands up, sighs, sniffles, wipes her eyes with the tissue. She grabs her cell phone off the charger plugged into the wall and sits down beside me again on the bed.

Now composed, she opens up a WhatsApp chat. "These are just some of his children. My brothers and sisters. There could be more." She scrolls through what appears to be hundreds of messages over the past several weeks. "I've been giving them updates on Elijah as I got closer to him."

"Holly, this was all so dangerous." I sigh. "I wish you'd talked to me."

"I did what I had to do," she says. "I wanted to feel like I wasn't alone in this. I have their support. They trust me, and I trust them. We're the only people who understand what it's like to have this man as our father." Holly's face twists with pain. "All I ever wanted to do was stop Elijah from having any more children with random women. I was miserable growing up without a father. I don't want anyone else to go through that."

"Holly, maybe we should go home," I suggest in the gentlest way possible. "We can't stay here."

Holly's eyes widen. "You would let me go home with you, after all I've done?"

"I understand you had your reasons. And while I may not trust you with my daughter right now, I want to make sure you're safe. I'm so grateful you called me here. I know you didn't want to hurt Lissa. And I believe you, about Elijah. It all makes sense, and..." A surprising amount of emotion pricks at my nose, bringing me close to tears. "And I suppose I'm one of his victims."

She nods. "I know."

"We need to explain all this to the police and to Jace and Rick," I tell her. "From there, we can figure out what to do."

Holly grabs the formula and heads toward the door. "That's a good place to start."

When I stand, I'm surprised that my legs can support my body. The revelations over the last hour have left me reeling but not broken. Perhaps I'm not processing the full extent of what happened, or maybe I always knew. Ever since that night, whenever I looked at Elijah, I felt sick. My body knew before I did. My body has reacted to the man every single time, but my mind blocked it out.

It's almost dawn. An ashen-yellow sun is attempting to rise through a collection of thick clouds darkening the sky. Rick will be wondering where I am. It hits me then that Elijah was so evil to call what we did an affair right to my husband's face. Hot rage floods my veins. Holly is right. This man needs to be stopped.

At the car, I'm strapping Lissa into her seat when I see a flash of dark movement through the window. My head

The Nanny's Secret

snaps up. A man with broad shoulders, dressed in all black, a mask over his face, is grabbing Holly.

He gets her in his grip and yanks her away from the car. Holly screams, her limbs flailing as he drags her back. I slam the back door and race around the side of the car, reaching for Holly, attempting to grasp any part of her I can find in the dim light, but the man is faster. He scrambles away with her across the parking lot, a cupped hand clamped over her mouth.

I scream for help. Terror roots me to the spot. Holly's eyes—huge, wild, and sparking with pleading—meet mine. She's out of my reach within a few seconds. And then they both melt into the shadows.

Chapter 35

The air is cool around me. I immediately close the car door and lock it so that Elijah—I'm assuming it's him—can't get to my daughter. She'll be fine in the car seat for a short amount of time. The sun isn't up yet, and it's a chilly dawn.

I grab my phone and call the police, telling them where I am and what's happening.

"I think it's my neighbor. Elijah Johnson. He's wearing a mask, but I think it's him. Please come quickly." Panic makes my voice quiver. As I'm talking, I walk to the edge of the parking lot, my gaze traveling around the area, searching for Elijah and Holly.

The 911 operator talks calmly, taking down all the details and asking me to repeat myself when the words come out garbled.

"Perhaps you should wait in your car, ma'am," she suggests.

I glance at my car, where Lissa is sleeping soundly, and

The Nanny's Secret

then I hang up. What is Elijah doing to Holly? To his own daughter?

Rather than lock myself away in the car, I hurry to the motel reception to see if there's anyone who can help me. Even though I screamed for help, no one left their rooms. But I wonder if they're also calling the police right now.

The reception is empty. Cursing the owner for leaving me stranded, I hurry around the side of the building to where the woods meet the perimeter. I'm panting. I take a moment to calm myself and then use the flashlight function on my phone. Here the trees are dense, blocking out the early-morning sun. Through the darkness, right by the tree line, I see a scurry of movement. It's faint because it's far away, but it has to be them.

I scramble toward them, switching off my phone light to remain undetected. I have to use the dim light of dawn to guide me. My gaze flicks back and forth between the ground and straight ahead. I don't want to lose sight of them, but I don't want to fall either.

All the while, Lissa's safety is probing in my mind. Am I doing the right thing? Am I making a mistake? I remind myself that the police are on the way, and they'll handle things. For now, I have to take the risk for Holly. If he kills her, I will live with that guilt forever that I didn't at least make the effort to save her.

I slow down to move more quietly. If the attacker is Elijah, then I already know he's much bigger and stronger than I am. I need a weapon. I duck low, searching for a rock, something with weight. There's a piece of broken tree branch. I grab it. It's better than nothing. Now I have a weapon and the element of surprise, if it comes down to something physical. Though I don't know if he's armed. I can't predict any of it, and the terror claws at my insides and constricts the air in my throat.

Tree limbs whip at my arms and cheeks. Pine needles scratch my ankles. My heart thrashes against my ribs. This is taking too long. I have to get back to Lissa. If I don't find them in the next thirty seconds, I'll have to go and leave it to the police to save Holly.

I listen closely for the wail of sirens, but there are none. Maybe the police won't use them, not wanting to spook the attacker. I glance over my shoulder, praying I find flashing red and blue lights, but I'm met with dark trees closing in behind me.

And then there's the softest brushing of leaves, followed by a twig snap. I follow the sound, watching where my feet fall, avoiding any twigs or crunchy leaves that will reveal my location. The branch is heavy in my right hand. I raise it slightly, ready to strike.

Holly's scream pierces the silence. Then I hear a thud that makes my stomach roil.

Around the next pine tree, they come into view. Elijah, still in his mask, has his hand clamped over Holly's mouth to keep her quiet. She flails against him, tugging at his clothes, scratching and trying to kick him. He's too strong, too forceful.

He uses his weight to push her down before smacking her in the face. I wince. Holly goes limp, and he pulls her up into his arms, disappearing behind the trunk of a large tree. I stop, afraid he'll hear me. And then they're gone.

The Nanny's Secret

The moment I lose sight of them, I lose all bearings. I can't keep track. I stop walking, listening, ears straining. I hear nothing but silence and the faint rustle of leaves. There's barely any light and no sound.

I take a few cautious steps forward. There's no snap of a twig, no rustle through a bed of leaves. No whimper from Holly or panting from the attacker.

I can either go a little farther, try to catch up to Holly and somehow get her back to safety, or I can return to Lissa and wait for the police. But what if they're too late? If I want to save this girl, I need to act fast. I look back and forth. I can't afford to hesitate. I know what I need to do.

Chapter 36

I charge deeper into the forest, branches thrashing against my face and arms, leaves tussling under my feet. I don't care anymore if Elijah sees me. He probably knows I'm following him anyway.

Lissa is locked in the car, I remind myself. He can't get in. She's safe. Besides, I know Elijah is too distracted by hurting Holly to do anything to Lissa. Elijah isn't someone who actually wants his children. He just wants to know they exist.

"I called the police," I shout. "They're on the way. Stop running now. You can't get far. These woods aren't that deep, and there's a highway on the other side."

My voice bounces off the trees, whispers through the wind, rushes through the leaves. If the assaulter had a gun, chances are he probably would have used it by now. I'm not leaving this damn forest without Holly. Adrenaline surges through my veins. I'm fueled by my determination, my legs powering full steam ahead.

The Nanny's Secret

I skid to a grinding halt in front of a ditch and see a lump lying in the center.

"Holly?" I pant, wiping the sweat off my neck with the back of my hand.

No response. I drop to my knees and peer into the ditch, fingers splayed across the dirt.

Holly's limp body is sprawled out like a starfish. She's lying face down, and a smear of dirt is across her left cheek. Leaves and pine needles are stuck in her matted hair. Her right shoe is missing, and her shirt is torn at the bottom hem.

Beside her rests a big rock, slightly smaller than a football and with the same oval shape to it. A splatter of something dark, wet, and sticky is on the side of the rock.

My eyes dart through the dim light, searching for shadowy shapes. Holly's attacker is nowhere to be found, unless he's hiding behind a tree, waiting for the perfect opportunity to pounce and club me over the head too.

I drop to my knees and push two fingers into the soft flesh underneath her chin. She's alive, but her pulse is weak. I angle her head slightly better to allow her to breathe more easily. I gasp when I see the trickle of blood oozing down the side of her temple. Her hair is matted there with sticky blood. There's a gash, almost the width of a finger, sliced through the side of her head, just above her temple.

I rip off another piece of her already torn shirt and clamp it to the head wound to blunt the bleeding, but the cloth is thin, and it immediately soaks through.

"Holly, wake up." I gently tap her cheek. "Stay with me, honey. Can you hear me?"

No response. Her eyelids don't even flutter. Her mouth is gaping open, her head tilted back. I lean forward and place my ear close to her mouth. Her breath is low and slow, but it's there, puffing against my skin.

I tear off another piece of her shirt and press it to her wound. The garment sticks to the blood. It will have to do. Now I'm going to have to figure out how to get her out of this ditch and back across the field to the parking lot.

Hopefully, the police have arrived or will be arriving soon. Holly is petite and probably only weighs about a hundred pounds, but I still need to prepare myself to haul her through the woods. I still don't know if she has any other injuries that I need to be mindful of. It's too dark in the woods to inspect her properly.

I anchor my legs on either side of her legs and rub my palms together. I pull my hair back into a ponytail with an elastic band I always have on standby wrapped around my wrist.

I take a deep breath and lean down, making sure to bend with my knees and thighs and not with my back. I cup my hands around Holly's torso, and with a grunt, I get her front half lifted off the ground about five inches before my fingers slip from around her and she drops with a thud to the ground.

"Shit!"

Holly doesn't react, which isn't a good sign, but as long as she's breathing, she's getting oxygen to her brain. Maybe she's just knocked out. It was a huge rock, after all.

The Nanny's Secret

If her attacker bashed it against her skull, she could have internal bleeding, swelling in the brain, and other dire issues.

I try not to think about that nightmare. The quicker I get her out of here, the faster she can get the proper medical care she needs. Lissa is still in the car, hopefully still asleep. I can do this.

I try again, shuffling around to the side of Holly's limp body. She's going to be dead weight, but I need to stir up enough strength within myself to do this. Adrenaline powers through me in that moment, and I try a different approach to picking her up.

I put one hand under her shoulder blades and the other under her legs and carefully lift her, holding her like I might cradle Lissa. Holly's arms and legs dangle, but I've got a decent grip on her. I start moving, shuffling through the woods, panting hard, face hot, my shirt clinging to my back from the sweat.

When we make it to the clearing, the motel comes into view like an oasis. I've never been more relieved to see a decrepit motel in my life. My arms are shaking. My knees start to buckle. My body wants to give up and drop Holly, but I'm almost at the finish line. Just a few more steps. One foot in front of the other. I can do this. I keep my eyes trained on the grass, watching out for any holes, but it's easier for me to get across the field if I'm not looking straight ahead and only concentrating on what's on the ground directly in front of me.

After what seems like an eternity, I reach the asphalt, stepping over the curb, arms trembling with the effort and the weight, sweat trickling down my back and chest. My back aches, and my spine is near snapping.

I lift my eyes and scream.

My car is still in the parking lot where I left it, but the back door is open. I set Holly down at the curb and run to the car. It's surreal, like I'm watching this nightmare unfold from a different place in the universe. My head is too heavy for my shoulders. My feet are made of concrete, yet I'm still able to charge across the parking lot to the car in seconds.

I whip around the back and lean in. Lissa's car seat is empty. Terror seizes me. I can't breathe. I can't see. The motel lights blur, becoming a fuzzy mess in front of my eyes. The sky is spinning at a million miles an hour. The ground is opening me up and swallowing me whole.

"Lissa!" I shriek, and the pain and fright and fear in my voice rips from my throat, blaring out into the crisp night air.

I search under the seat, comb through the front seat, open the liftgate, and with my knees and palms to the ground, crawl around each side of the car, looking for her. I know it's a fruitless effort. Elijah returned to swipe my baby after dumping Holly in a ditch. I was wrong. Lissa was never safe here. Panic rings through my ears. Lissa is gone. My baby is gone. She's *gone*.

Chapter 37

The sound of a baby's cry—one that I recognize—is music to my ears. Lissa shrieks from behind me. I spin around and find Elijah standing at his car. His mask is off. He stares at me, his eyes hard in the dim light.

He's on the other side of the parking lot, near the exit to the main road. The passenger door is open, and Lissa is clutched like a football in his arms. He bends over and shoves her into the back seat.

I'm running. Running until my lungs burn, until my thighs ache, ponytail whipping behind me. Lissa's muffled wails carry from the open car door.

Elijah straightens and slams the door. His back is facing me. On light footfalls I close the space between us, hurtling toward him like a bullet launched from a barrel. I reach my arms out in front of me to cushion the blow and shove him as hard and as strong as I can.

It's like I've gained a second wind from the universe,

like the universe is on my side, is going to give me the strength and stamina to see this through to the bitter end. All I care about is getting my daughter out of the hands of this monstrous predator.

Elijah is a wolf in sheep's clothing. I can't believe I trusted him, allowed him into my home, shared dinners with him, and confided my pain and grief. I slam into Elijah's shoulder. He startles and stumbles backward, teetering on his heels. His arms sway at his sides as he rocks to regain his balance without falling, but I barrel into him again like a human wrecking ball. He crashes to the pavement with a heavy thud.

He lets out a searing groan as his palms slice across the gritty asphalt. I'm at the car door before he can get up again, fingers fumbling with the handle. As soon as I clutch it, pain scorches through my scalp. Elijah grasps my ponytail in his fist and yanks me backward. My head is thrown back. I'm vertical, the gray clouds floating above, the only witnesses to this hell I'm living through.

Where are the police? They should be here by now.

"You should have stayed in your own lane, bitch," Elijah growls in my ear, his breath hot against my skin.

I shudder as an icy chill jogs up my spine. I scramble to my feet. He grabs my shoulders, and I throw my elbow back and pound it into his side. Elijah wails and topples backward.

"I'm going to kill you," he roars.

I knee him in the groin. His eyes burn with rage, and he grits his teeth, balling his fists. I try to duck the first blow, but his swing is too quick, too powerful. He clocks me in

The Nanny's Secret

the eye socket, right where the top of my cheekbone begins. I hear a crunching sound.

Stars and fire explode behind my eyes. Pain rips across my face, reverberates in my jaw, tremors down my spine. I gasp, but no air goes into my lungs. I fall to my knees as a swell of nausea churns in my stomach. I scratch at the air, still gasping. My throat finally opens, and I gulp the crisp air into starved lungs.

My lips are numb, and splotchy patches of light and darkness are whirling across the eye that Elijah struck. I'm down but not out. I reach for the blurry shape of him as he's racing to the driver door. He gets it open, but I grab his ankle, wrap my fingers around it, and sink my fingernails deep into his flesh until he cries out. He shoves his leg forward, hammering his foot into the ground, trying to wrench free. I rake my nails down his skin until I leave red tracks—jagged, bleeding scratches. Getting my DNA under his skin, burying his DNA under my nails, just in case.

"Get off me, bitch." Spittle flies from his mouth, dribbling like the fine threads of a spiderweb down his bottom lip.

"Give me my baby back." I choke on every word, barely able to breathe.

"It's *my* baby too," he grunts.

"*She*, not *it*," I snarl and punch the back of his knee as hard as I can. He topples forward, hitting his face on the side of the door on the way down.

I rush in the opposite direction, trying to get to Lissa, but he's too fast. His arms reach around my waist.

"I'm going to fucking kill you. This is all your fault, and you won't get away with it," he growls.

I see red. "No, *you're* the one who won't get away with this." I throw back an elbow then lift my right leg, hitting him in the crotch.

He grunts, and his arms loosen. I climb out of his grip, turn around, and slam my sneaker into his abdomen. Finally, Elijah folds, falling onto his back.

While he's still down, I climb him like a tree frog. My knees dig into his chest and stomach. He's panting hard, trying to kick free, bucking his hips. I use one knee to keep his legs down while I take his wrists and pin them to the ground.

But he's too strong, and I'm too tired. He jerks his arm up because I can't hold both at the same time on either side.

Once he wiggles one arm free, the next soon follows, and before I can think of what to do next, those big hands reach up and coil like a snake around my throat.

He squeezes, pressing his fingers deep into my windpipe. When I sputter, he grins. I try to cough, but there's not enough air. Elijah watches me, his white teeth flashing under the dawn light, too bright in the darkness between us. He howls with cackling laughter. His lips twist.

Nothing but madness is behind his eyes. He digs deeper, tightening his hands around my throat until my vision fades in and out. Blackness cuts through my eyes. Everything is blurry. I try to focus on the image of Elijah's face, his manic laughter, his outstretched lips, and his wide-open mouth, but I can't. I'm struggling to breathe. I can't think. My survival instincts kick in, and my hands flail toward the hazy round shape of his face.

My nails find skin and drag across the surface. A cheekbone. A lip. A jaw. I scratch and scratch, hearing him shout in pain. His head thrashes back and forth against me. I still don't have any air. I'm light-headed. My eyes pulse, burning, the blood vessels swollen and tremoring, ready to burst. But my fingers still inch upward from his chin, crawl across his nose, upward to his cheeks, and then I find his eyes. I feel him pinch them shut, protecting them from the invasion of my fingers, but I dig and claw and try to pop his eyes out of his sockets.

He has no choice. He releases one hand from my throat. I gasp, reeling back, my own hands going to the sore, tender area. I'm choking, drawing in air. My lungs and throat are on fire. I taste the metallic tang of blood in my mouth and in the back of my throat. He lets the other hand go.

Elijah is on his knees, trying to scurry to his feet. His eyes flare with hatred. I'm still dizzy and struggling to get enough air, but I back away from him, toward the car door. He can't see my hands, but I have them clutched over the handle.

I time it right so that when he's in front of the door, I swing it open and smash it into Elijah's face. Blood splatters from his nose, bright red and dripping down his face, into his mouth, getting between his teeth, staining them maroon.

He cups a hand over his nose and rocks back on his heels. Revenge and rage coil around me like smoke. My eyes burn from being suffocated. My throat is sore and aching, but the darkest, deepest, most suppressed anger boils to the surface, rising from me like heat.

"And *this* is for me, for Lissa, for Holly, for Emma, and every other woman you've used and abused." I close my fist and bring it thundering down onto Elijah's face, hearing the bones in his nose cracking under the sharp edges of my knuckles.

His eyes roll back in his head, and he drops like a domino to the ground, his skull smacking into the asphalt.

Lissa is screaming in the back seat, arching her back, not quite in the harness, dangling half out of it. I reach for her, glancing over my shoulder to make sure Elijah isn't behind me, ready to strike another blow that could be fatal this time.

He's unmoving on the ground. His eyes are closed. He's knocked out cold, but as I look down at his hand, his thumb twitches. He might not be out for long.

I untangle the baby from the seat strap and grab her, hugging her close to my chest. She smells like salt and urine and formula and sweat. I kiss her damp cheeks, brush my fingers through her fine blond curls.

"It's okay, baby," I whisper, rocking her in my arms, backing away quickly. "Mommy's here now."

The wail of sirens finally screeches in the distance, and I see the flashing red and blue lights splashing off the trees and the road in front of us. I continue to back away from Elijah in case he leaps up for one last attempt to hurt me or Lissa. He's desperate now. He knows his life as he knew it is over. But a man like him would try to take someone down with him. Selfish to the core.

My throat opens, and sobs of relief and exhaustion explode from my chest. Raw and throbbing, in competition with the blaring sirens.

Chapter 38

The light-up mobile spins in a slow circle, splaying pastel-blue, canary-yellow, and cotton candy colors across the walls and the rails of Lissa's crib. She's sprawled out like a starfish in my favorite pajamas, a pink zip-up footie set with orange, sunset-colored cloud print across the soft fabric. I watch her tiny, delicate chest rise and fall. Every now and then, her eyelids flutter, and I smile, wondering if she's dreaming, hoping that the images in her head are of pleasant and familiar things.

I stroll across the darkened bedroom and peel back one of the curtains to glance across the street. The only light on in the house is coming from the living room downstairs. I called Emma Johnson in the hospital this morning to see how she was feeling, and she told me she and baby Zander would get to go home today.

My chest tightens when I realize how close Elijah came to kidnapping Lissa. If only Rick had warned me his key fob was faulty and didn't always lock on the first press. I figured out that was how Elijah got into the car. But I'm still not sure why Elijah wanted to take Lissa and what he thought the next plan would be.

What I've gathered is that Elijah followed me to the motel that night, guessing correctly that I would lead him to Holly. He'd then gone back and parked at the hospital before making the twenty-minute walk to the motel with his ski mask in his pocket. He wanted to get rid of Holly and was prepared to do anything. Parking at the hospital gave him an opportunity to force Emma into giving him an alibi. And she probably would have. Even now, when I spoke to her on the phone, she sounded so oddly emotionally detached that I think she actually believes Elijah will be coming home to her.

It's my own speculation that when Elijah's plan to kill Holly backfired, he went after Lissa out of spite. He wanted ownership of my daughter, and he wanted revenge on me for stopping him from killing Holly.

"Knock knock."

I turn around and see Rick standing in the hallway. He gazes down at Lissa's sleeping form and smiles. Then he turns to me, and his smile fades, replaced with a tight expression of anguish, along with, as much as I hate to admit it, pity.

"Hey," I whisper.

"Hey," he whispers back. "Is she sleeping?"

I nod.

He opens his mouth to speak but then closes it again. Rick now knows that I was raped, that I didn't make the consensual decision to cheat on him. I did let Elijah into the house when Rick wasn't there, but I didn't do it thinking that Elijah and I would do anything non-platonic. But maybe I had leaned on another man for emotional support rather than talked to my husband. For that, yes, I am guilty.

I clear my throat, breaking the uncomfortable silence. "I think Emma just got back from the hospital. I need to see her."

Rick's forehead creases, and he glances at his watch. "Right now?"

"Lissa's asleep, and you are home for the night. I figured now was the best time."

Rick pads into the room and clutches the crib railing, peering in. A gentle smile brightens his features. "She's so cute when she's sleeping."

"She's always cute."

Rick swivels. His eyebrows pull together, and he looks so sad that it tugs on my heart. Our marriage is strained, and it might take some adapting to get it back to where it was, if ever. I've made my peace by letting him take his time, giving him his space to process everything that's happened.

He takes a deep breath and looks at Lissa again. "Aud." His voice shakes, and a sob explodes from his chest.

"Hey." I lean over, wrapping an arm around him. "Hey, it's going to be okay."

"You are the most important person in this world to me." He grabs my hand, squeezing it tight. "And I've cared more about making money than being with you. When we

The Nanny's Secret

lost the baby, I pulled away from you, and I allowed that... that *psychopath* to prey on you while—"

"Don't," I say, tears gathering in the corners of my eyes. "Don't. I'll cry again, and I've wasted enough tears."

Rick pulls me into his arms and holds me tight. "Audrey, I'm so sorry. I'm sorry I thought you had an affair with him. I feel so guilty—"

"It's okay. We didn't know."

I think of Jace walking into the room, seeing his mother being raped but not knowing what he was seeing. I think of Holly, carrying the emotional weight of knowing who Elijah was while trying to gather evidence of his crimes. I think of Emma, living with him, being manipulated and controlled by him, carrying his children until the physical burden of it almost killed her. The tears come, and they don't stop. Rick cries into my hair too. And once we're both done, it's like balm on my soul.

We slide out of the room and crack the nursery door. I have the monitor in one hand. Sometimes I find it difficult to put it down. Gently, Rick pries it from my fingers.

"Rick, I spoke to some of the other women today."

We head down the hall.

"Oh yeah?" he says.

"Yeah. They want to be part of the victim accounts," I tell him.

"Well, that's promising."

Three days have passed since Elijah's attack on Holly. Both Elijah and Holly had been taken to the hospital after the police arrived. Elijah was treated for a broken nose and a mild concussion before being released into police custody, where he still sits, without bail. His formal charge is attempted murder, but I'm working on getting the victim statements and stories from the other women Elijah has preyed upon. It might take a while, but I'm optimistic that my efforts will pay off in the end to keep Elijah behind bars where he belongs.

Holly is still in the hospital, undergoing treatment for a severe concussion. Her head injury was more involved, and the doctors advised us she may need rehabilitation after she wakes up to get back to normal daily function. I want to call her mother and let her know what happened, but I can't get into Holly's phone, and her only emergency contacts are Rick and me.

Luckily the assault charges against Rick were dropped and his job is safe. The police decided to focus their efforts on Elijah, something I think I have Detective Stalks to thank for.

We step into the bedroom, and I grab a tissue from the dressing table to wipe my eyes. "Rick, there's something I need to say." I take a deep breath. "I know he violated me, and I... I'll have to unpack that. But I will never regret Lissa. I'm sorry if that makes you uncomfortable. If... If you don't want to be seen as her father, I do understand. I should have told you. I fucked up, Rick. I'm so sorry." My voice cracks, and a lump forms in my throat.

Rick's chin quivers, and he tightens his jaw. "She'll always be my daughter, not his. I'm her father. I am the one who will raise her."

I nod adamantly. "Of course. She's your daughter,

The Nanny's Secret

always will be. Nothing will ever change that. She'll never grow up around Elijah. She'll never know him."

I'm not sure what I'll tell Lissa about Holly. I know I want Holly and Lissa to have a relationship. Perhaps we'll cross that bridge when the time comes.

Rick plants his hands on each hip and takes a deep breath. "I've also been thinking about something else."

"What?"

"Now this is just a suggestion. You don't have to make a decision right away. Take as much time as you need to think about it, but..." He chews his bottom lip and looks at the wall. "We should move."

"Move? Away from here?"

"Not the city, necessarily," Rick clarifies. "Your business is established, and I have work." He pauses and adds, "Although I'm going to be cutting my hours back significantly. No late nights, no weekends. That will be family time."

"So you want to sell the house and move to a different area of town?"

Rick shrugs. "If you're up for it."

I don't even need to think about it. "I think that's a great idea."

"Yeah?" Rick's eyes brighten.

"Maybe we could stay in the school district for Jace."

"I'm sure he'd appreciate that."

Things with Jace and me are still a little frayed, but he cried in my arms and apologized for everything that happened in the aftermath of the viral picture. I forgave him and told him we each learned a valuable lesson. He promised to never do anything like that again.

Rick grounded him for the rest of the month and told him he would be on laundry and dishes duty for another month after that. Jace took the punishment stoically and without complaint. He knew he was in the wrong, and he was responsible enough to own up to it.

Little by little, our family will fill in the cracks of our broken foundation.

I pat Rick on the shoulder. "We can start looking at houses and talk to a realtor about getting this house listed." I sigh. "I need to see Emma. She was Elijah's victim, too, and I... Well, I just need to see her."

Rick gives me a solemn smile. "Take your phone and call me if anything happens."

"I will."

***

Over at the Johnsons', I stand under the porch light and knock three times. I hear a shuffle of movement on the other side. The lock clicks, and the door peels open a crack.

Emma is standing there, blinking at me in surprise. "Audrey? What are you doing here?"

"I just wanted to come talk to you for a few minutes. Sorry, I know it's late, but I promise it won't take long."

The door opens the rest of the way. Emma is holding the baby, who is sucking at a bottle. She steps aside. "Come in."

"Thank you. He's so cute, Emma."

The Nanny's Secret

She gazes down at her newborn son with pride glazing her eyes. "Thanks."

She seems brighter than the last time I saw her. There's color in her cheeks again, and her hair has been brushed. I follow her down the hallway into the kitchen.

"Do you want any tea, coffee? I think I have some donuts—"

"No, don't worry about it, Emma. We can just talk. You need to rest."

Emma nods, walks toward her living room. She sits down in a recliner, and I sit down next to her on the couch, folding my hands in my lap.

Emma's eyes are bloodshot and a little puffy. She looks like she's been crying. She's not wearing socks, and I can see that her ankles are swollen.

I cross my legs and lean forward. "We need to talk about Elijah."

Emma turns away. "The weather is nice today. It's been so chilly recently. Colder than usual, don't you think?"

A creeping sense of sadness worms its way up from my stomach.

"Emma, have the police explained what Elijah did?" I ask.

She bites her bottom lip. Then she says, "Yeah, they came here." Her grip seems to tighten around Zander.

"Emma, your husband raped me and many other women. He tricked women into carrying his child. He's a predator, and you need to start rebuilding your life."

The baby finishes his bottle, and she lifts him to her

chest and begins lightly patting his back. "Well, I have a lot to do with the kids and everything."

"Okay," I say. "Do you need any help?"

"Help with what?" Her expression switches to startled.

"I don't know." I frown. This conversation is a lot harder in real life than it was when I practiced it in my head on the way over. "With finding a good lawyer."

"What would I need a lawyer for?" she asks. "If you're implying that I'm going to leave Elijah, I'm not." Her jaw is firm, her lips pressed together into a tight seal of absolution.

"Emma—"

Her eyes narrow, a storm brewing inside them. "Did you only come over here to try to convince me to leave my husband?"

My spine snaps up straight. "What? No, Emma. I just wanted to come check on you. You lived with a violent man. I'm worried about you. I came here to see how you were doing, what your next steps are going to be."

"My next steps are going to be up to my bedroom to go to sleep. After that, I'll wake up and get my kids ready for the day. I'll make their lunches. I'll feed my baby. I'll cook, clean, and do laundry. I'll restore order to this house, *my* house where I live with my family. The way I always do, the way I always will."

"But—what about—I mean, Elijah is in jail," I say.

She shrugs. "One day he'll come back. Anyway, why should I uproot my children from their home and everything familiar to them just because my husband made mistakes?"

The Nanny's Secret

I let out a derisive snort. "Mistakes? He's a *violent* man. You can't stay with him. You just can't!"

I'm on my feet before I know it.

"You don't need to worry about me. I'll be just fine." She stands.

That's it, the cue that I've worn out my welcome. I don't want to stay here a moment longer.

By the front door, I try one last time. "Listen, Emma. I'm not trying to insult you. I didn't come over here to try to upset you. I just want to make sure you're going to be okay. You deserve so much better. You are smart and young. You have a lot going for you. Elijah has a lot more children than just yours. Of all ages. Some of them are even adults now. He will never change. He's being charged with attempted murder and rape. Look at these bruises. Look at the marks on my neck. He did this, and he's not coming home, Emma. Do yourself a favor and get out while you can."

"In sickness and in health," Emma says weakly.

She's broken. She isn't the same woman I helped with a banana pudding just a few weeks ago. Her eyes are glazed over and indifferent. Maybe she's in shock. I hope for her sake and the children's sake that she snaps out of it sooner rather than later.

"Good night, Emma. Take care."

I turn around and hear the door close behind me, but I don't look back as I walk across her lawn, back to my house across the street.

Chapter 39
HOLLY

The door to my hospital room swings open. Audrey walks in, pushing a stroller containing Lissa and a bunch of beautiful red roses. A teddy bear is clutched under her arm. The teddy bear is holding a plush heart. I'm surprised not to see Jace, but Audrey and I want to discuss the upcoming charges against Elijah, which Jace probably shouldn't listen in on.

"Hi!" Audrey declares breezily as she sets the bouquet on the table beside my bed and hands me the teddy bear. "How are you feeling today?"

I shuffle my way to a better sitting position, resting my shoulders against the propped pillows behind me.

"A little better," I admit. "I went to physical therapy, and my arms don't feel like jelly anymore. The doctor says I should be able to go home within the next week or two. I have an appointment with a cognitive therapist and a speech therapist, too, and maybe I'll test out some writing

The Nanny's Secret

to see how my skills are to this point. I'm kinda slurry, aren't I? And yesterday I forgot the word *dairy*."

Audrey pushes her foot to the brake on the stroller so it won't slide across the linoleum floor. "That all sounds very promising."

"Yeah, and I can't wait to get out of here and have a cheeseburger."

Audrey laughs. "I can bring you snacks if you want. Anything you want actually. Just make me a list."

"Really?"

"Of course." She beams, nodding.

"Thanks so much."

Lissa stretches out her arms and reaches her dimpled hands toward me, sitting forward in her seat.

"Can I hold her?"

Audrey gives me a cautious look. "Are you sure you're up to it?"

"Yes. I've missed her so much." There's a catch in my voice as the last few days come flooding back. I've been thinking about Lissa as my half sister for a while now, but after everything, that bond between us has strengthened even further.

Audrey removes Lissa's harness strap and hands her to me.

Lissa immediately gets cozy, nuzzling her face close to my chest. I kiss the top of her forehead. "Hey, little sis."

"Now that I know what happened, I see how much you two look alike," Audrey admits. "I think it's great that she'll grow up with such an amazing big sister. You're so strong, Holly. You'll be a fantastic role model for Lissa."

Audrey's kind words bring tears to my eyes. "It means the world to me that you would say that."

It's been a long road, and I still have a long way to go before everything goes back to normal, both in my life and my body. But I refuse to give up.

Audrey sits down in the chair next to my bed and rakes her fingers through her hair. Her cheeks are flushed pink.

"So, have you told your half siblings about Elijah's arrest?" she asks.

"A few on the phone, a few over text," I say. "They're all shocked but glad he's getting his comeuppance at last. It's good to have them to talk to."

"I'm glad you have that base," Audrey says.

"What about you?" My heart beats faster as I look her over.

Audrey crosses her legs and cups her hands over her knees. "I created a Facebook group about Elijah. A support group of my own." She smiles sadly. "Some of the women have agreed to press charges."

I breathe a sigh of relief. "That's going to strengthen our case. Thank you so much for everything you've done while I've been in here."

Her eyes sparkle. "Of course. That's what family is for."

Family. The word makes me warm all over. It's wonderful to have her on my side after all we've been through.

I kiss the top of Lissa's head. She smells like lavender baby soap. I inhale a deep whiff of it.

"I do have some other news." Audrey picks at her

thumbnail and lifts her eyebrows toward me. "A woman called Tracey came up to the house while I was working in the front yard the other day. She lives down the street, but I've never really spoken to her before. Well, she heard about Elijah's arrest. She came to tell me she's pregnant and Elijah is the father. She heard what Elijah did to you and why, and she came over to talk to me about it. She's worried about what will happen next. I told her we'd do what we could to support her."

"Wow." My stomach clenches. "That's awful. I hope she'll be okay."

"I'll check in on her," Audrey promises. "But she'll be okay because I am, and you are, and we will all go on with our lives. He won't break us. Never. We're going to put that man behind bars, and we're going to live our best lives."

So much fire lights her eyes that I believe her.

"Have they... Have they found any videos yet?" I almost don't want to know the answer, but I have to ask.

Audrey closes her eyes and slowly opens them again. "Detective Stalks searched Elijah's house. A USB stick was found." She balls her hands into fists and lets out a long breath. "I'm on it."

"I'm so sorry, Audrey. Are you okay?"

I hug Lissa closer to me, wanting to protect her from all the cruelty of the world. She snuggles up to me, babbling. I gaze into my baby sister's bright gray eyes, and the tension floods out of me.

Audrey straightens her back. "I'm fine. I'm just glad the evidence will make sure that evil man will rot in jail. Fuck him."

"Fuck him," I agree. Then I look down at Lissa guiltily. I laugh at the silliness of feeling guilty. Lissa can't understand what I'm saying. "If only I'd been conscious to see your mommy slam a car door into your daddy's face."

Audrey laughs then. She places a hand on her stomach as the manic giggles take over. I join in, and Lissa's tiny head bounces around. Then Audrey leans over the bed and places a hand on my forearm. She gives it a quick squeeze. I know what it means. It means we're family now. I nod, and my eyes fill with tears.

My mom has been in and out of the hospital to visit me, and it wasn't easy explaining to her everything I did. But I did it for my mom and for Audrey, who I will always see as a sort of big-sister figure. And even though my body is beaten up, I don't regret a single second of it. Because I did it. I finally removed an evil man from the world. He will rot in jail, like Audrey said, and we will live on free and happy.

We're a family now—me, Lissa, and Audrey. And all of the half brothers and sisters that Elijah Johnson abandoned.

"You know, I'm a little tired," I say, passing Lissa back to Audrey.

"You want us to go?" Audrey asks.

I nod. "But you'll be back tomorrow, right?"

"Of course." She smiles brightly. "Oh, and I want to meet your mom."

"Okay," I say. "Maybe when I'm out of the hospital, we can all go out for dinner."

She smiles. "I'd like that."

Audrey places Lissa back in the stroller and waves as

The Nanny's Secret

she rolls it out of the door. Slowly, I close my eyes. With a sense that everything is finally going to be okay, I let sleep take me.

*

Thank you for reading THE NANNY'S SECRET. If you enjoyed this book please consider leaving a review, they are so useful for other readers and help authors so much.

And if you like to continue reading my books, I suggest checking out THE SECRET FAMILY.

Sign up to my mailing list to stay in touch!

About the Author

SL Harker was raised on Point Horror books and loves thrills and chills. Now she writes fast-paced, entertaining psychological thrillers.

Stay in touch through her website: https://www.slharker.com/

Join the mailing list to keep up-to-date with new releases and price reductions.

Also by SL Harker

The New Friend

The Work Retreat

The Nice Guy

The Bad Parents

The Secret Family

The Nanny's Secret

Printed in Great Britain
by Amazon